PRAISE

"'Every murder is a parable,' quips Jim Feast's Eleanor Marx. Indeed. Feast's hyperreal historical collage manages to feel equal parts Columbo and Perec, and to graft Nicholas Meyer's *The Seven-Per-Cent Solution* into Max Ernst's *Une semaine de bonté*. I'm already greedy for another of these ripping father-daughter whodunits."
—Jonathan Lethem, author of *The Arrest* and *The Feral Detective*

"In *Karl Marx Private Eye*, Jim Feast not only engages us intellectually, but as the readers unravel the mysteries, there's a good laugh every few pages and gorgeous descriptions of the hotel, the clothing, and the food of the time. It's a very witty, fast-moving story with a terrific ending. If you like detective fiction, you'll love this book."
—Barbara Henning, author of *Just Like That* and *Digigram*

"Feast writes with a poet's pen, a humorist's wit, and a Dashiell Hammett knack for detective fiction. When a series of dastardly crimes are committed amidst Bohemia's health spas for the rich, you don't need a Hercule Poirot when you have the improbable team of Karl Marx and a teenage Sherlock Holmes on the case. Luscious writing that evokes the politics and culture of the era."
—Peter Werbe, author of *Summer on Fire: A Detroit Novel* and member of the *Fifth Estate* magazine editorial collective

T0026303

Karl Marx Private Eye

Jim Feast

Karl Marx Private Eye
Jim Feast © 2023
This edition © PM Press

ISBN: 978-1-62963-993-2 (paperback)
ISBN: 978-1-62963-997-0 (ebook)
Library of Congress Control Number: 2022943297

Cover design by Drohan DiSanto
Cover art: "Eleanor and Karl at the Hunter's Ball" collage by Allan Kausch
Interior design by briandesign

10 9 8 7 6 5 4 3 2 1

PM Press
PO Box 23912
Oakland, CA 94623
www.pmpress.org

Printed in the USA.

For Nhi Chung
珍贵的宝藏

Ah! It has been a terrible struggle. I sometimes wonder how I have lived through it all. I firmly believe that owing to my long intercourse with cats, I have acquired, like them, nine lives instead of one.
—Eleanor Marx to Jenny Marx, January 15, 1882

Viens, mon beau chat ...
Retiens les griffes de ta patte,
Et laisse-moi plonger dans tes beaux yeux,
Mêlés de metal et d'agage
("Come, my dear cat ... draw back your claws and let me dive into your beautiful eyes, a mix of metal and precious gems")
—Baudelaire, "Le Chat"

The cat, she said, was the tiger's teacher. Originally the tiger couldn't do anything, so he turned to the cat for help.
— Wang Shiqing, *Lu Xun: A Biography*

They danced by the light of the moon,
    The moon,
    The moon,
They danced by the light of the moon
—Edward Lear, "The Owl and the Pussy-Cat"

Chapter 1

August 1875, Karlsbad, Bohemia

Always her dreams had the same form. Someone speaking. No one, nothing, visible. A sentence and then the visual segment to follow. Not more than a single sentence. This evening, Eleanor heard, "You must follow a movement across a row of dreams." Then repeated, nearly repeated, "You must bleed across a row of dreams."

Then the visual. Something was taking place in a courtroom.

They say when you sleep you revisit, in a confused way, the previous day. Last evening, the table talk in the Tři Lilie Hotel dining room had turned on a criminal case. When they had ordered and were waiting to be served, their friend Dr. Cranky, sitting on Father's right hand, had pushed his acanthus-decorated plate across the white tablecloth and picked up the *Rheinische Zeitung*. Glancing down the brief Notices column, he'd read the following tidbit:

"'Felix Kugelman'—given with one *n* by the way, where I believe there should be two—ahem, 'Kugelman, the assassin who escaped two weeks ago, was seen last week in the Black Forest on the road toward Darmsbach. He had set up a blind above the Lovers' Catapult Bridge but was flushed from there and is about to be apprehended. It is believed he is now concealed in the city. The police say his capture is imminent. If he is caught in the next couple days, as seems likely, he will be executed at dawn Saturday. Since he was already under sentence of death when he escaped, no further trial is needed to prosecute the outrages he committed while on the run."

Setting down his coffee cup, Father had stroked his side whiskers. "So it is in Bohemia. Because of prior offenses, the criminal is denied a trial; the paper denies him his right name. The only thing he has been correctly informed of is the hour of his death."

Cranky had added, "Which is the one thing a man would perhaps rather not know."

Eleanor had recalled to them the line in Lord Byron's *Don Juan* referring to the transitory passage of military glory, apropos a press notice.

Cranky, professor of modern poetics in Berlin, had then recited a passage in which the bard talks about Jack Smith, who rated a descriptive clause in a list of the fallen in battle. After giving the clause, Byron continues:

> I've said all I know of a name which fills
> Three lines of the dispatch in taking 'Schmacksmith'—
> A village of Moldavia's waste, wherein
> He fell, immortal in a bulletin.
>
> I wonder (although Mars no doubt's a God I
> Praise) if a man's name in a bulletin
> May make up for a bullet in his body?

Hearty laughter all around. Such had been the end of the night, and this sad thought may have been the cause, along with the oppressive heat, of her disturbing dream.

As Eleanor had slept, her dream self stood at the dock in a British courtroom. In front of her were four scarlet-robed, bewigged judges, who leaned forward to shush the crowd, which was especially disturbing because its whispering talk was mixed with odd grunts and cries. Peering more closely, Eleanor saw that interspersed among the typical court spectators were dressed-up animals: here, a she-wolf in the hooped skirt of the last century, there, a pious marmoset in a Roman collar. Strutting self-importantly down the aisle came a red-coated, red-shelled lobster, a repeater grasped awkwardly in his claw.

Each of the judges had the woolly face of an owl.

She had to defend herself. She stuttered, reaching vainly for what she wanted to say, looking for the right words.

Byron, whom she admired so much, touched on this form of speechlessness in *Don Juan*. Haidee and Juan had the perfect romance, and it took place, had to, outside of language. Juan only spoke Spanish, Haidee only Greek, as if the truest emotion could only blossom in silence. And so, too, to speak most deeply of her own innocence, her purity, she had no words.

In the dream, Eleanor stood there dressed in black, the sweat cropping around the roots of her hair, behind her ears where she had dabbed perfume, and moistening the hair in her armpits. Wetting her lips as if preparing to talk, but only able to smile what sister Laura called her Italian smile. In Vasari, there's a story about Leonardo. He employed jugglers, mimes, players of strange airs, all that was rare and *amusant*, to keep that magical smile on the Mona Lisa's lips.

Wetting her lips a second time and touching a whisker. There was a fragment of mirror that lay on the courthouse floor, and from it she caught sight of her cat's face.

With that surprise, she woke. The air was muggy, though a listless breeze was shivering the curtain, throwing a Japanese screen of shadows across her dresser and scattered sheets. Her shift was sticky, the bedclothes wet as with spray.

The room was tiny and spare. Her small bed, extending from the right wall, divided the room in half, leaving only a small passageway at its foot. On the door side sat a small oval writing table with chair and a washstand plus ewer. Her dresser stood in a splash of sun on the window side.

Pouring some lukewarm water from the ewer into a basin, she splashed her brow, took up the washcloth, and soaped her face, arms, and upper bosom. Even this tepid water was refreshing. After rinsing and toweling off, she went to her dresser. There, neatly laid out in a row, were various calling cards, tickets, and invitations that made up her social calendar. Today there was nothing but a dull visit to Lady Maple, the wealthy Britisher, but tomorrow was the Hunter's Ball and Masquerade. It was a fancy-dress Karlsbad custom in which the women disguised themselves as prey, though their masquerading might go no further than wearing a feathered mask. The men were hunters, sporting flap hats or horns around their necks.

She so wanted to go, but Father had not yet given his approval.

Below the list of engagements, which was a short one, as she and father were returning to London in a few days, were letters to be answered. On top was that from her fiancé, Prosper-Olivier Lissagaray. Behind these received letters, neatly folded and scribbled on both sides, were two replies to Lissagaray. She didn't know which one to send.

Their situation was at an impasse. What had begun as her schoolgirl crush on the older man, who had already distinguished himself by fighting in the Paris Commune, turned into rebellion against her judgmental, straitlaced father, who had at first forbidden her from seeing him. Year by year, three years now, she had whittled away her father's resistance. After all, Lissagaray was no idler or sponger in the way of so many Communards exiled in London. He was writing a learned, passionate history of the uprising, for which she often served as a research assistant. However, these past few years of working together on the book had not been good for their engagement. Olivier had so many crotchets, she said; she was so flighty, he said; yet neither sought to end the relationship: he perhaps desiring not to sever his connection to her "famous" father, she not wanting to give up the only emotional tie she had outside her family circle.

She composed her first reply fresh on receiving his letter, which, along with endearments, included a list of work that they would have to do straightaway on his book when she returned to London. She wrote plainly that she had decided to break off their engagement. Their relationship was too one-sided, she said. A day later, she rescinded that decision and wrote an epistle that informed him she couldn't devote so much time to helping him. She had her own work. She remained divided over which to mail, each representing something definitive and necessary but distasteful. The letters sat before her like two bottles of poison.

Eleanor rang for the chambermaid, then sat on the bed edge, pulling the pantalets over her shift.

Swandra came in, large-boned with a florid, pink complexion and russet hair, on which sat her pert, tilted maid's cap. Quite a contrast to Eleanor, with her swarthy complexion, bushed-up black hair, and introspective brown eyes in a sincere, balanced face.

Swandra began attiring Eleanor, accompanying her ministrations with piquant observations on the hotel's other residents. Though the maid's knowledge of the beau monde in Karlsbad was extensive, she presented it promiscuously, jumbling together a duke and an organ grinder or putting a countess hard at elbows with a pot girl.

"Baron von Siemens," Swandra began as she brought out the corset, "was walking behind the water wagon as it laid the dust on the western approach to our jeweled city this morning. The plug came out of a cask and wet his trousers. He had to retire in a most undignified manner."

"Don't tug so hard."

"Pardon, my lady. Oh, and the wife of Minister Haupt

thought she saw a flea in her rooms and screamed so loud that the maid spilled tea on the dear husband."

"Oh, dear."

"The manager contends the flea was a speck on her lorgnette."

"Do preparations go forward on the Hunter's Ball?" Eleanor asked.

"Swimmingly. How many petticoats will mademoiselle have?"

Eleanor let the clammy weather rather than fashion determine the answer, but more thought had to be given to which blouse to wear. Not that she had much wardrobe. The choice was between a cream or tan shirt. Nothing would do but to try on each alternately before the glass until, impulsively, she left on the cream.

Swandra prattled on as she combed Eleanor's bushy hair. This was her morning ritual: one hundred strokes. Since, like most women, Eleanor was only able to wash her hair once a week, these brushings helped evenly distribute the oils.

Taking up an historical perspective, Swandra was discussing the toilette of various ladies of fashion she had waited on over the years. Eleanor listened with great satisfaction.

In her daybook, Eleanor had wondered why middle-class women at the spa (like herself) were so taken with observing the aristos. Perhaps it was simply opportunity. The nobility had exclusive restaurants and clubs, but when it came to places of public resort, such as the promenades and the pump room, there was a catholic mixing of all classes.

Just as young children are fascinated and slightly uncomprehending of adult behavior, so older children—adults—fussily watch over the behavior of their betters, who seem to be living on a still more adult plane. This was the vice for which Emerson chastised others. As she quoted him in her commonplace book:

> Insist on yourself; never imitate. Your own gift you can present every moment with the cumulative force of a whole life's cultivation; but of the adopted talent of another you have only an extemporaneous half possession. That which each can do best, none but his Maker can teach him.

When she finished dressing, she dismissed Swandra, pressing a token into her hand, and proceeded to her father's room. She listened at his door, heard no sounds inside, and decided not to knock. Father was following a twenty-one-day plan to deal with his liver problems and skin eruptions. He was scheduled to be up at five thirty. If he had overslept, it would be graceless to discover him.

Instead, she walked the stately corridor to the blue, carpeted staircase and descended to the mezzanine, from which one could look on the lobby with its lovely red Persian carpet rolling out to the ornate wooden doors. The lobby, like all Karlsbad hotel lobbies, was overstuffed. This one, with its elephant-foot umbrella holders and plentiful ostrich and peacock feathers, gave the place the air of a children's zoo.

She thought most guests would be breakfasting. At this hour, the lobby was usually as placid as a Swiss lake. Instead, it was filled with chattering guests. Women were clustered at the front door while a knot of men stood to one side, blocking entrance to the dining room. Among them she recognized the equestrian instructor and the bandmaster, the first in high boots and riding togs, the second in garish mauve pants, a knee-level dark-green coat, and a top hat. Also on hand was her young acquaintance Sherlock, who had joined them at table a few nights. The sixteen-year-old could be seen everywhere except in the company of his parents. He was something of a beanpole stripling, being near six feet in height, with gray eyes, the nose of a hawk, and the thin lips of a gambler. She scanned the crowd but saw neither Father nor Dr. Cranky.

Eleanor hurried down the last few steps and came up, full tilt, on her British acquaintance Mrs. Smallweed.

"What is it?" Eleanor said. "What has taken place?"

Smallweed rubbed a runny nose. "The pump room has been closed. The police have cordoned it off. Oh, dear, there must have been an outrage perpetrated. A rape is likely."

Mrs. Smallweed was no more than her name implied: short, and always dressed in black, wearing widow's weeds for her departed husband. She was always moving, and with her thin bones and sharp angles, she looked as if she had been carved out of granite and then animated, resembling a female version of the Commodore whose statue jumps off its pedestal at the end of Mozart's *Don Giovanni*.

Like an old rain barrel, she was given to leaking on the slightest change in the atmosphere. Now, as she spoke, she dabbed at her eyes. "I've been crying."

"Why did they close the hall?"

"It's rumored that terrible cutthroat Kugelmann appeared. Oh, if he ever approached me." Smallweed swallowed, grew paler at the outrage the ruffian was performing on her in her fantasy, then keeled over, toppled like a pillar diddled by Samson.

Eleanor, forced to fold the matron in her arms, caught her under her pouter pigeon bosom and looked around for assistance.

Two stout Germans sprang to help her, one settling the woman on a handy couch in the lobby and the other making to fan her.

"Rum show, that," said Sherlock as he came up at her elbow. "The woman seems to have been strongly affected," he added. "Beastly affair."

As Eleanor viewed it, Sherlock, to hide his inexperience,

talked like a blade a few years his senior. Even so, she liked to talk to him, because he was as full of news as a mailbag.

"What do I hear about them shutting the waters?" she asked.

Sherlock gazed at the stairway.

The pump room was where one went to drink the health-enhancing water that flowed from a natural spring. A water cure was one-third guzzling, one-third soaking, one-third steam. All this was highly sociable; even the bathtubs for women were set beside each other so conversations could proceed along with soaking.

Every spa was recommended for a certain ailment: Baden-Baden for rheumatism, Hévíz's medicinal mud for bone diseases, Karlsbad for gout and nerve disease. Roulettenburg had its supporters as the best place to treat your kidneys. So, while there were manifold amusements from masked balls to concerts to gaming rooms, the springs were the paramount draw.

With a city so dependent on fluidity, turning off the taps of the pump room was a serious matter. Eleanor asked, "Did they really shut the pavilion?"

Sherlock came back, "The public has not been let in on this, but—Miss Arbuthnot, step aside here—I can whisper the whole thing. I have a particular chum here, a member of the fusiliers, who gave me the up-down."

Smallweed had awoken and jammed into their group. "What has gone wrong?"

Sherlock: "Nothing short of murder."

"Murder," Smallweed yelped, and she spouted more tears.

People turned to the group, swarming around them as if they were bees and the three stood at the entrance to the hive. One asked, "Has someone been killed?" Another: "What do I hear of murder?"

"Damnée," Sherlock swore, "never open your mouth to a petticoat."

"What is it? I have to know," said Smallweed, pressing into the youth's face.

"I'll enlighten everyone," Sherlock said to the band collecting around him. "The pump room opens officially at seven a.m., but the ticket taker makes it available to her special friends, such as Professor Cranky or anyone who has a ready hand with tips. This morning, a crowd showed up for an early dose: Cranky, plus the American millionaire Henry Van Winkle with his wife and their maid. The attendant escorted everyone inside, and then, finding the help had failed to replenish the store of glasses last night, she excused herself to run across the street to the storage building for fresh supplies.

"She bustled inside and saw no glasses had been left on the sideboard, so she ran upstairs to the room to unpack more cups. Cranky, who had followed her to help out, also ascended the ladder. Then they heard the maid's bloodcurdling scream. They rushed downstairs, Cranky far ahead. When she exited, she saw Cranky flying down the street.

"The fräulein made her way into the pavilion, where she witnessed a gore-bespattered scene. The millionaire, stabbed in the gut, hung limply across the basin, spouting blood into the water. He was half-naked, shirt off and trousers half-undone. Molly lay on the floor as if she had fallen onto the knife, which had disappeared. The attendant, who has nerves of steel—she served as a nurse in Versailles in the late war—tried to stanch the blood of the maid, but her light had already been quenched."

As unaware as a bowling ball that had sent pins flying, Sherlock prattled on while a number of ladies in the circle followed Smallweed into oblivion and had to be supported by stationary males.

Eleanor, who was of sterner stuff, interrupted, "I can't believe Professor Cranky, who is mild as a mouse—"

"Both Cranky and Mrs. Van Winkle," Sherlock explained,

"were apprehended. With such chaos, it's safer to arrest everyone who might have had a hand in the mischief."

Eleanor talked through her rising terror. "But why would Cranky, who didn't even know these people . . ."

Sherlock deduced further: "For that matter, why would Mrs. Van Winkle elect to murder her husband, to whom she had only been married for a few weeks? Even though, as I've heard, they did have a public spat in the lobby of the Ludwig Hotel."

"Who could have done it?" Eleanor asked over butterflies fluttering in her stomach.

Sherlock answered, "Whoever did it was a bloody-minded rascal. They say Van Winkle was filleted like a mackerel, with his blood turning the white marble floor black."

Eleanor had not been a nurse in the war and felt a cold creeping up her limbs, like the first sign of frostbite. Everything went dark.

$\sim$

When she awoke, she found she had been transported to a settee next to a rotund pillar, where she was being fanned by a quartet of accommodating gentleman as if she were a soup tureen. She felt mixed emotions: chagrin at being so lily-livered, yet some satisfaction as she made out the handsome riding instructor, Von Pelt, among the creators of the tepid breeze. She gazed at him through her misted vision.

He wore a short, black topcoat and half-length black pants stopping at the brown leather riding boots, everything impeccable. He was clean shaven, leaving visible his delicate chin, slight nose, and coolly curved lips. His black eyes were shining with insouciance. He was touching his riding switch to his leg.

She roused herself, saying, "Sorry to—"

"Don't speak, Miss Arbuthnot," she was chided.

She sank back, letting herself lie silent as if she were on a beach, with the waves of speculation about the murders lapping her ears.

"It must have been Cranky. No woman could have throttled the old banker. *Mein Gott*, he was built like an ox."

"I'll never believe that. Cranky is a professor, a man of the head, not a strong-arm bandit."

"What is the man's subject?"

"He teaches modern poetry at Humboldt University."

"I take back what I said about his delicacy. Modern poetry, egad. Why, he might as well hold a chair in pornography."

"And didn't the American cause a disturbance at the Ludwig hostelry when he accused his wife of infidelity?"

"In the open crowd."

There were only three men talking. Von Pelt had gone to fetch her a glass of water, which he now placed delicately in her hand. She smiled up, seeing him through a glaze as if now she were a ham.

It was seldom anyone waited on her. Certainly not in her home, where she was generally the one on duty. She remembered fondly her few sick days, such as when she came down with jaundice. What with a poor diet, the noxious atmosphere in their neighborhood—at that time they lived in Soho on the filed edge of the London slums—and the cigar trailings in the upper corners of the room as father sat plotting with fellow German émigrés—she might have been witnessing a convocation of locomotives in the rail yard, they gave off so much smoke—it was no wonder she got sick and turned yellow. She kept abed for weeks, indulged and pampered. She took to writing notes in a strange script, consisting of cylinders, spheres, and triangles. When her sister Jenny questioned her, she announced she was turning Chinese. Even when she had recovered, her elder sisters would still call her the Empress of China.

"Would you like more water?" the noble equestrian questioned.

The universal cure.

"No, I just want to go upstairs and rest for a few minutes."

She got up and, still a bit wobbly, was supported to the stairway back in the entrance room, which suddenly had become the scene of a new commotion, this one caused by her father, who came running into the room from outdoors, looking a fright. His collar was ripped out, buttons missing from his waistcoat. He wore a maddened look in his eye.

He rushed to her side. "Are you all right, Tussy?"

"Certainly, why certainly, Papa. The news of this violence merely upset my nerves," Eleanor replied.

"Your nerves! What about mine?" he came back angrily.

"Why, what do you mean?" Eleanor asked, startled by his vehemence.

He replied, "I was just assaulted, a knife pressed to my throat, by that escaped mad killer."

Chapter 2

Eleanor's father told the story, starting with his first stir-rings in bed that morning.

Nearly nodding off after the hotel man's first door tap, he was aroused five minutes later by the second rapping. As a health resort hotel, the Tři Lilie was well programmed to handle reluctant or backsliding patients.

Nicknamed the Moor due to his dark skin, Arbuthnot had lost the shapelier figure of his youth, now bulking out due to his sedentary lifestyle. The well-trimmed beard and coiffure of his younger days had been replaced by hair scrambling up above his head and a beard plushing out to boisterous size. The beard had gone gray, but his mustache was streaked with black.

Dressing precipitously, almost without knowing, Dr. Arbuthnot found himself briskly striding along Alpenstraße past the Grand Hotel Pupp with his mind, figuratively, in tatters. Single thoughts plunged awkwardly back and forth without awakening any train of association or sustained reflection.

He ran into Dr. Cranky, also up at this ungodly hour and on his way to the pump room to pursue a flirtation. Arbuthnot decided to accompany him partway. They chat-ted about the murderer Kugelmann, whom they had been reading about in the gazette. Though Kugelmann's guilt was obvious, seeing as he had carried out his assassination in broad daylight, the nature of the crime was ever unclear. Had he shot his ex, who was in a carriage with a politi-cal leader, a notable opponent of Serbian independence?

Or was this a political assassination gone awry when the Serbian shooter had accidentally killed his former fiancée while aiming at the notable?

Arbuthnot left Cranky near the pump room, chuckling to himself at the man's slightly comic intrigues, but his grin turned to a bitter sneer when he encountered the American millionaire Van Winkle and his entourage. He knew the man for a dastard, who evenhandedly bilked stockholders, oppressed workers, and cheated the US government, as he had by selling shoddy weapons during the Civil War. Van Winkle's armaments firm was ready to supply any of the reactionary crowned heads in Europe, including the Austrians, who had recently been putting down small protests in Serbia and Bohemia.

Arbuthnot returned to his thoughts, making his way down to the river, which bisected the city. He paused on his ashplant, musing himself while listening to the musings of the rippling water. He nodded to a few acquaintances and people from the hotel who passed.

Karlsbad ran along the River Teplá, with most of its buildings crammed along the north bank, being arranged on three parallel winding streets in the limited space between the water and the abutting mountains. The pastel-colored houses gave the streets a garish liveliness. Looking up from the river, the steep perspective made it appear the rows of houses sat on each other's backs, being as closely placed as flowerpots on receding shelves.

Arbuthnot's musings ended when he saw a brace of police with their double-breasted greatcoats and train-porter hats going quickly by. What was up?

Wouldn't you know it? Like a boy running after a fire truck, Mrs. Smallweed was trotting behind the squadron. Here was the human Baedeker he needed. "Is something afoot?" he asked.

"Can't stop. Can't stop."

"Why the police?"

"It almost gave me the vapors," she told him, a tear springing from her eye. "Kugelmann is on the loose. A desperate desperado. He was seen at the zoo. Then he rushed to the pump room. The police have cordoned it off."

"Why would he go to the zoo?" Dr. Arbuthnot asked.

She rushed off without answering. There was nothing for it but to go back to the pump room. After all, one of the attractive features of the spa was scandal in small doses, taken in due proportion with the other nostrums one imbibed.

He crossed past the baroque Maria Magdalene Kirche, whose façade, like a puffed-out chest, jutted out from the main structure, which itself vaingloriously began with two onion-topped towers. He went down a number of streets to the pavilion. When he entered the avenue, he found a sizable crowd behind a group of police guarding the entrance to the pavilion. He ran into his little friend Sherlock, who took him aside by the window of a toyshop and recounted what he had learned.

Here, they parted company, Sherlock heading to his hotel and Eleanor's father joining the other spectators, all of whom shared humankind's universal penchant to study the unrevealing facades of a building in which atrocities had been enacted. They stood passively attentive, like cows staring at a passing bicycle.

The oaken door set in the glass-walled pavilion—overall, the building resembled a greenhouse, with milky panes on the lower portion and transparent ones above—was the one dark place in the broad front. It seemed to glow as if charged with phantom electricity.

Not satisfied with the distant prospect and remembering that his personal physician lived hard by in an apartment across from the pump room, next to the toyshop, Eleanor's father entered the building, hoping to glimpse the murder scene through Dr. Feckles's upper-level windows.

Dr. Feckles was not one of those society doctors whose income depended on drawing up weight-reducing plans and water cures. He was a local doctor who took on occasional seasonal patients but mainly served the local gentry and nobility. He had a third-floor apartment right off the pump room but saw patients in his clinic.

Dr. Arbuthnot toiled up the stairs, pausing on his cane for a breather at each landing. He looked out a window and saw that now the police were forcing the crowd back down the street, leaving the area in front of the pump room free of people. Arbuthnot thought worriedly not of the murder, but of the fate of his friend. Though he and Dr. Cranky sometimes parted for the night on the worst of terms, having gotten seriously embroiled in a dispute over the day's varied political currents, it never lasted. The pair would sail off to bed, each with his jaw jutting out like a bulldog's, only to greet each other next morning with the smiling faces of porcelain pugs.

Cranky had his foibles, such as his overpaying of compliments to the pretty maids and house girls, but he was no blackguard. His hand was ideal as a pen holder, not as the wielder of a poniard. Although Arbuthnot was staying only a few more days, there was still time to help his friend.

Eleanor's father was admitted to the rooms by Dr. Feckles's wife, who said her husband had already left on his rounds. The guest requested the use of her window. He went into the sitting room, which directly overlooked the pump room, and waited as the maid threw up the sash. He glanced around the room, which was backed on all sides by filled bookcases. A heavy armchair sat to one side, next to it a table holding a pitcher of water and a pair of spectacles.

Compressing his bulk, Arbuthnot leaned out, noting the street was deserted due to the police blockade. The flat roof of the pump room, directly at his level, and the building's upper sides, except for a brick cuff on one wall, were composed of a mesh of oblong glass panes, muddied by rain wash. Looking down through the lower, translucent wall, he could make out three silhouettes: policemen, no doubt.

His attention shifted, caught by an intermittent sound as if a chisel were scraping at his building's facing. On looking down, in a split second of bewildered disorientation, he thought a mirror had been attached to the side of the structure, for he was staring at his own face, or, well, his younger face.

Taking hold of himself, he grasped he was looking into the eyes of a man, a kind of rock climber, who was slowly squeezing his way up. The man's hair was long and tousled, sparked with dirt and held in place by the bandanna of the Italian red shirts. There was a hunter's blade seized between his teeth.

The climber placed his hand on the sill.

Instinctively, Dr. Arbuthnot cried out, "Murder, bloody murder," even as he struggled to pull his wedged bulk from the frame. Since he was facing the avenue, it might be assumed his cry would alert the police investigating across the street, but, as happens so often, those he addressed neither recognized nor responded to his summons, while unintended listeners—the women behind him in the room—created a commotion, which he heard as a scream, a flutter, and something crashing to the floor.

He broke free and spun around (a bit ponderously) to see Mrs. Feckles in the arms of the saucer-eyed maid. A second twist of his torso and he was again facing the window, as the convict—he recognized him from newspaper drawings as Kugelmann—pulled himself through the window. Arbuthnot, taken aback, stared incredulously at the man advancing as if he were a jellyfish that had popped out of the sea, sprouted legs, and was walking his way.

The convict was a massive man in his torn garb, which appeared to be a bath attendant's uniform. He looked exhausted, shattered, and dirty, yet still with something of an air of magnificence, like the gentlemen robbers in Schiller or those in the Bard's *Two Gentlemen of Verona*.

The villain shakily shifted the blade from his teeth to his hand, but just as Arbuthnot backed up to shield the women, he dropped his weapon to the floor. The convict soon followed, collapsing, his left arm thrown straight out above his head as if he were pointing at the bookcase or, was it, proffering a final salute.

The maid, who might have understood she was out of immediate danger, took this opportunity to also faint, so that Arbuthnot had to turn and catch her as she (and Mrs. Feckles, who was in her arms) fell. Thus it was when the gendarmerie eventually arrived; they found him wrestling with the weight of two women whom he was trying to bestow on a couch.

Later, Arbuthnot learned Kugelmann had probably been hiding in a building in this block, possibly a promenade room used by those who had just quaffed their healing waters. From there, he must have stolen his uniform. Inadvertently surrounded by police on all sides, he seized the opportunity of a momentarily deserted street to climb up this building, perhaps thinking Dr. Feckles, who had been his physician years gone by, would offer him succor. However, finding the apartment occupied by a stranger, Kugelmann's strength fled, and he gave up the fight.

~

Having delivered himself of this narrative, which if they weren't standing, would have kept most listeners on the edge of their seats, and which elicited a few new tears from Mrs. Smallweed, the crowd mostly broke up for other pursuits, leaving a few diehards, Sherlock, Smallweed, and Eleanor.

The four agreed they would meet for lunch in the hotel dining room to discuss these events. Eleanor retreated to her room to rest and repair her hair. Holmes said he was off to reconnoiter the scene of the crime. Smallweed went outdoors to fan herself, and Eleanor's father seated himself in a capacious chair, toying with a cigar that he wasn't allowed to smoke, ashplant propped up at his side. He stroked his beard and ran over the day's events, wondering in particular why someone would have wanted to murder Van Winkle.

As he saw it, the choice was between love and glory. Either his new wife had lost control of herself in some love spat or a benighted Serbian anarchist, who blamed the arms maker for supplying his oppressors with weaponry, had broken in upon the financial privateer.

His cogitations were cut short by the reappearance of little Sherlock. "I thought you were off," he said, not happy to have been interrupted.

"Yes, I was. But, dash it, there was something I meant to take up. Perhaps in privacy, if you prefer."

"What's this then?" Arbuthnot asked apprehensively.

"I feel I caught you in a little lie. It's naught but a slip, but I like things straightforward among gentlemen. I'm keen-eyed for facts, don't cha know."

Arbuthnot felt seriously uneasy at the boy's approach. It was probably nothing, and he was probably attributing more powers of detection to the young Sherlock Holmes than he deserved, but the solid fact was Eleanor's father was traveling under an assumed name. Some years ago, he had written an incendiary pamphlet defending the workers who had died fighting for the Paris Commune, and this had gotten him in hot water with the authorities.

Only these meddling, copper-headed British Philistines could not grasp the heroism of the Parisian rabble. When it was surrounded by invading Prussians, the city tried to hold off the invasion; unfortunately, General Trochu, who early on was in charge of the Parisians, was a noted bungler and had not properly armed or trained the workers guard. As the Prussians kept up the pressure, the regular French army and the leaders of the government fled in panic. Rather than surrendering, defense was taken over by street militia, directed by a quickly elected interim group.

Instead of applauding, the French government, which was hiding in Versailles, was scandalized when the Parisians set up their own government, electing workers and militiamen to the chief posts. The Versailles leaders, dogs to the man, were so frightened by this ultra-democratic government that they made an alliance with the Prussians to invade the city. The rebels were overcome and massacred.

What could Arbuthnot do but lift up his pen to defend this lost cause?

This pamphlet had two dire consequences. He was banned as an agitator from visiting continental Europe, and his own home became a way station for exiles. With his pamphlet offering such a ringing defense of the people's democracy, every Communard fleeing to England, the country of refuge, beat a path to Arbuthnot's London residence, where they not only claimed meat and drink and perhaps a night's lodging as a small recompense for whatever heroic exploits each visitor claimed to have done holding the last barricade, but, worse yet, the young men among them began casting wayward eyes over Arbuthnot's three marriageable daughters. By this time, Eleanor's two older sisters, Jenny and Laura, had already married French exiles, and Tussy seemed on the verge of going the same route.

So, when they moved farther back in the lobby, Arbuthnot was fully expecting Sherlock, who had previously mentioned his brother was a police commissioner, was going to "blame and shame him," as the saying went, by saying he had found out his true identity.

"So, what is it you want to accuse me of?" Arbuthnot said point-blank.

"Well, the first thing you said when you started your narration of the pump room, you said the man pressed a knife to your throat, but when it came to the point where you were holding up the ladies, you said he fainted dead away."

"Yes, well?" Arbuthnot returned.

"You didn't tell the truth, my dear fellow."

"But I didn't lie either," Arbuthnot defended.

"Well, if it was not a lie," Sherlock asked, a bit perplexed, "what the deuce was it, then?"

"A flourish. A literary flourish."

Chapter 3

When Eleanor came to lunch that afternoon, she felt the diners had erected a hedgerow. Her father and Mrs. Smallweed each sat behind a newspaper. It was the afternoon edition, likely to have notice of the morning's crime wave.

Sherlock came in right behind her. "I say, they seem to have put down the portcullis."

At that barb, they lowered their papers. Each, it seemed, with a different wince.

"Anything in there we don't know?" Sherlock pressed as he pulled out Eleanor's chair. Then he reached over her shoulder and straightened the silverware, which was out of alignment. "That's better."

Mrs. Smallweed answered, "Nothing we haven't already ferreted out for ourselves." For emphasis, she double-folded her journal and scooted it under the table.

The hotel dining room was long and thin, only two tables across, with various service areas taking up one side. The inner wall was sectioned off by fluted columns as if frames for the large oil paintings placed on them, which showed either peaceful forest vistas or a stern general with or without charger. The outer other wall was windows. While at night the chandeliers were lit to drive back the darkness, in the afternoon the curtains were generally drawn to ward off the light.

The waiter came to take their orders, either noting them down or, for those on restricted regimens, Arbuthnot and Smallweed, ticking them off on a card.

Sherlock then came back to the convict. "There's a great deal of balderdash in the public's opinion that Kugelmann was hiding on the pump room roof. A half-starved fugitive decides his best means of hiding is to scale the slippery side of a glass building? Don't sell me a dog."

Mrs. Smallweed remarked, "I think there's a ladder they use to get up on the roof."

"But what do you think happened?" Eleanor put to Sherlock.

"My solid principle—we talked of this with Cranky a couple days back, when I mentioned the Dupin principle, you'll remember, miss—is to go based on only what we know. Only use the facts that face us."

"And what are they?" Mrs. Smallweed interrogated.

Sherlock glanced significantly at Dr. Arbuthnot. "We know from Dr. Arbuthnot that at, say, seven thirty a.m. Kugelmann was clinging to the side of a building. He ascended to Dr. Feckles's rooms," another glance, "put a knife to your father's throat, and fainted away."

Arbuthnot heavily frowned as Sherlock spoke—a lot of frowns this noon, Eleanor thought.

"If he was half-starved, how did he manage to climb a building?" Mrs. Smallweed said.

Sherlock came back, "I say, I placed my words carelessly, though that doesn't often happen. I meant Kugelmann didn't have the strength to be foolhardy. And it would have been a reckless act to show himself on the pump room roof. However, if the circumstances shifted radically, as they did that morning, with *Polizei* swarming, fear and desperation might have propped him up, on his last legs as it were, as he sought a way to escape."

Arbuthnot put in his oar. "My young friend, you are a triple-dyed dummkopf. The very thing that gave Kugelmann vigor—the peril of police everywhere—gives the lie to your reasoning."

"How so?"

"You imply the assassin was stationed in the vicinity, nearby. He takes a notion to clamber up the side of the building. But how can he accomplish this? Even though the streets were clear, there are police just inside the building opposite. Clambering up a wall would make a stir."

"Maybe I didn't underline my principle strongly enough," Sherlock said. "What we know is that we have him between the second and third floors. I don't imply how he got there. We have to remain just there." He referred to something he'd said yesterday about detective fiction. "This was Dupin's principle also."

The appetizers came up and people picked them over. Once those were stowed away, the main course was served. Eleanor had a nice sausage, lying like the shaft of a cannon in a mishmash of corn and green vegetables. Her father was eating, as prescribed, the lighter chicken paprika.

The discussion passed to a new subject, not a new topic—for what other topic could there be except the killings? They talked of the high crime that put Kugelmann in jail in the first place. It was carried out in broad daylight on a Karlsbad bridge. One afternoon, Kugelmann had run up on the open coach of Freiherr (Baron) Colloredo-Mannsfeld and shot at him. The bullet grazed the baron's shoulder and killed his wife, seated beside him.

So had Kugelmann, who was an aristocratic Serbian nationalist, meant to kill the wife, who had been Kugelmann's fiancée and was purportedly stolen from him by the baron? Or had he been aiming for the baron, who violently opposed Serbia's independence?

For Eleanor, it was the political aspect that was uppermost. She voiced the opinion that Kugelmann was sick of the trespasses against Serbia's limited sovereignty and made a bold thrust for his country's liberation. She told everyone that she had read in the international press that "the Serbian cause was like mother's milk to Kugelmann, doubly so, in that when he hung at his mother's breast being nourished, his mother was probably humming a Serbian musical call to arms as a lullaby."

"Yes," Sherlock cast in, "a spoon-fed diet of propaganda—"

Arbuthnot interrupted, a bit uncouthly. "Not a spoon, my dear chap, but a nipple."

"A-hem," Sherlock went on, "but such parental preaching often causes the opposite effect from what is wanted, and the young person grows up despising his guardian's fanaticism."

"Yes, admittedly," Eleanor returned, "but in other cases the young man falls in with his parents' plans, having set his course toward their goals."

"There's not much evidence for that," the boy went doggedly on.

Eleanor's watchword was, there is always proof in the Bard, so she quoted Richard's speech in *Henry VI*:

> For I have often heard my mother say
> I came into the world with my legs forward
> Had I not reason, think ye, to make haste
> And seek their ruin that usurp'd our right.

She sat back. A difficult passage, but she brought it off, so she thought, with a nice flourish.

Dessert coming in, the subject changed again. This was the question of the relationship—if such there was—between the Van Winkles and Cranky. For if there was no connection whatsoever, how could they have acted so familiarly in the pump room?

Eleanor put in, "I can't imagine Dr. Cranky, who lived so much in the realm of the intellect, even knew of this money buccaneer's existence."

Just then Sherlock's mother appeared to shepherd him back to their suite for his afternoon lie-down. She was dressed in a costume full of flowers, with a garden of artificial ones pinned on as decorations as well as a large living bloom, as large as if a blue-winged bird had set down on her bosom.

A shy woman, she stopped behind her son's chair as he spoke, concluding for everyone that Cranky didn't know the Americans.

"There was one thing," she said timidly, offhandedly.

Everyone at table looked at her with a single stare.

"Mother, don't be getting on," Sherlock said in a perturbed tone.

"But I'm just thinking that Mary Van Winkle was at the spring book auction. The *Mirror* rotogravure had a piece about it. She was a highlight."

Mrs. Smallweed asked, "What auction was that?"

"At the Mayfair booksellers' event, last April. It led the society column. All rare and many pretty volumes under the hammer, as they say. A fine packet of pounds crossed hands at that sale."

"Why would she go there?"

"Mrs. Van Winkle is all about collecting manuscripts and first editions from the Romantic writers. She also dotes on Shakespeare, our treasure. That's where you fit Cranky in."

"He attends auctions?" Arbuthnot shot in. "Doesn't seem the type."

"I don't know what he does, but didn't he have a lot for sale, a lot of German and French Romantics, and didn't it fetch somewhere on the high end? Seems he's liquidating a lot of his holdings."

Before she had time to field more questions, she told her son they had to be moving along. "Father is waiting, and you know how he detests waiting."

Before leaving, Sherlock, as he got up, leaned toward Mrs. Smallweed. "Could I just snag that paper, if you're finished reading? There's a peculiar operation I would like to perform on it."

Chapter 4

The day before, Sherlock had been talking of the "Dupin principle."

The four—Sherlock, Arbuthnot, Eleanor, and Cranky—had become acquainted and had been dining together for nearly two weeks, using the meal as a time to exchange views on the day's events, based on what they'd been reading in the daily papers.

Sherlock had a boyish enthusiasm for crime fiction and had pressed on his friends a copy of a reprinted short story by E.A. Poe called "The Mystery of Marie Rogêt." After the piece had been circulated, he brought it up, hoping they would share his excitement.

Cranky admitted the detective Dupin was to his liking. "I mean, the man sits on the sofa in his Paris apartment and reads the newspapers. He doesn't have to stir out of his room, just apply a little literary criticism to the reporting. I imagine I could do the same myself. I'm good at hunting for hidden meanings in poems. I fancy these villains are not better than symbols at hiding behind what's going on."

Sherlock jumped in. "Dash it. You haven't caught the nub. Dupin doesn't simply sift through the newspaper for clues. He watches for what the press says about public opinion. Here's where Poe takes the egg. I'll read it." With that, he quickly found the relevant passage and read it aloud:

> Popular opinion ... is not to be disregarded. When arising of itself—when manifesting itself in a strictly spontaneous manner—we should look upon it as

analogous with the *intuition* which is the idiosyncrasy of the individual man of genius. In ninety-nine cases from the hundred I would abide by its decisions.

Each had their own reason for disputing this idea that an intuitive wisdom reposed in the public. Arbuthnot said bluntly, "There is no public. That's another symbol. The Parisian populace is variegated: petty tradesmen, small manufacturers with their hands, the riffraff underworld of Eugène Sue. No single opinion."

Eleanor disagreed with her father, saying almost wistfully, "Sometimes all these groups come together with one voice, but that only happens when they are faced with a calamity like being surrounded by Prussian troops."

~

While yesterday Sherlock had been discouraged by the lack of faith in his theory, expressed in tones that had made him almost feel his elders were having a laugh at his expense, today, in light of a crime, he went to his rooms with a renewed interest in Dupin's efforts and decided to consult the newspaper Smallweed had given him. He wanted to look through the article to see what it recorded of the public's outlook.

He took a chair in the sitting room, both his parents having retired to somewhere in the back, and spread out the journal on an end table. He found that the reporter had only interviewed a single representative of the public, Mrs. Smallweed!

The reporter asked her who she thought had perpetuated this outrage.

She replied, "Kugelmann, no doubt. Everyone but Molly and the millionaire had temporarily gone out of the room when they discovered the convict skulking by. He killed them to hide his presence."

Sherlock thought, *I might have saved myself the reading*

by going into the lobby and having gotten this opinion from the horse's mouth. Discouraged by the reporter's lack of interest in canvassing the general public, he next thought, *Maybe I should go on an eavesdropping expedition of my own to ascertain the public's view.*

So, after a suitable time, that which his parents insisted on as necessary for digestion, he put on his jacket and headed out to eavesdrop on his fellow spa habitués. He had no authority to question strangers, but he felt he could sidle up to people who were talking and discreetly listen.

He passed down the staircase to the lobby, empty except for the riding instructor talking to a festooned dowager. Sherlock continued outside and crossed the gravel path, moving between carriages, and quickly made his way downslope, passing through the Mill Colonnade, which was a walkway covered by a stone canopy upheld by Corinthian columns. It offered both welcome shade from the thick August heat and, when there were no other visitors, a haunting vista with an almost sepulchral quality. Up above on the roof, the twelve carved goddesses, one for each month, were so small they seemed to be withdrawing from the gloomy scene.

Sherlock's intention was to get to the little shops that led toward the pump room and loiter there, overhearing the comments of the window gazers. He had learned from a lobby attendant that the cleaned pump room would reopen at five. It was nearly that time now. He would casually listen in to those staring at a new shawl or some touristy crockery. Given the influence of place on thought patterns, the nearness of the crime scene would probably lead many tongues to waggle about the violent incident.

Could he have been more wrong? People at the display windows talked about—what else?—things they wanted to purchase or what they had purchased or how good they looked in the reflection from the glass.

With relief, he greeted being hailed by Sergeant Hubner. On the first day here, Sherlock had made his presence known at the police barracks. The name Hubner was given him by his older brother, Mycroft, seven years ahead of him, who had a post in the International Police Liaison Task Force. Last fall, as it happened, a security conference had been held at Karlsbad, and it was there Mycroft had become acquainted with the good sergeant, himself a transplant, a German émigré. Right then, Hubner was on the track of an embezzler and, with Mycroft's timely assistance, the villain was brought to ground, which saved the Tři Lilie Hotel a handsome sum. It was this good deed that had paved the way for the Holmes family's vacationing here at a reduced rate.

He greeted the sergeant, a sturdy young man whose muscles almost bulged out of the restrictive police uniform with its black pants and green suit jacket, which was laced with so many roped-over tassels, they could have been used to tie a boat to a pier. Although his hair was invisible under the pith-helmet-like headgear, which was topped with a spike, Sherlock knew that if Hubner removed his hat, he would display brown locks that were beautifully cut and combed like the lovely hair of young Goethe shown in drawings of when the poet removed his powdered wig.

Sherlock was anxious to get right to the matter at hand. "Have you been to the place of the crime?" he asked eagerly.

"Just going there."

"Perhaps I could accompany you a part of the way."

"To the door, no farther," the policeman cautioned.

"Wouldn't think of intruding on the investigation."

They mutually nodded at a pair of passing sisters.

Sherlock launched off. "There's talk of a public dispute between the Van Winkles. Shocking bad show, that."

"Talk?"

Sherlock held back from speaking, having already learned that Hubner sometimes took time over a reply.

"You know," Hubner now said, "every crime creates a miasma."

Now it was Sherlock's turn to parrot. "A miasma?"

Hubner explained, "I'm referring to the absurd speculations of the general public, which grow like hothouse flowers in their fevered imaginations."

"Delightful metaphor," Holmes said.

"I have poetry in my veins," Hubner told him. "Remember my staff room? You saw the portraits on my wall. Did you recognize those gentlemen?"

When in the room, Sherlock had noticed a wall of bearded patriarchs, which he took to be retired police chiefs. "Can't say I knew their names."

"Schiller, Goethe, Klopstock, all the top boys in the poetry line. In a way, they are more the fathers of their country than all the political humbugs such as Bismarck. The poets can read the hearts of the people."

"Are you a poet yourself, sir?" Sherlock felt prompted to ask.

Hubner frowned as if found out. "I dabble a little, mere artistic dabs."

They nodded together at a passing couple.

"But," Sherlock began, trying to get the officer into a less flighty strain, "I heard the millionaire accused his wife of adultery."

A mutual nod to a passing military gentleman.

"You couldn't ask for a more ludicrous scene," Hubner said, finally becoming informative. "How the dispute started I can't say, but Van Winkle and his wife were exiting the dining area of Ludwig's when the louse began upbraiding his wife, calling her out for her treachery and infidelity. She was hot, too, and said something like, 'Who do you dare accuse me of seeing?' The old man spins around, happens to see one of our most esteemed officers, Captain Von Pelt, making his way into the establishment, and points to him."

"And you call this ludicrous?"

"The old man was flailing. He named the first man who crossed the threshold." Hubner knit his brows as a stern gentleman passed and then went on. "The public sees this contretemps as the cause of the murders. Others think Kugelmann was hiding on the roof, tried to sneak away, was seen, and so struck out to cover his location."

"Doesn't seem plausible," Sherlock commented.

They stopped in front of a closed shop so Hubner could finish his thought. "I don't know if you surveyed the scene of the outrage. Behind the pump room is an open square from which you can climb a ladder to the roof. From that square, there is a door to a small corridor that runs in a hall beside the pavilion to a street door. So, the public think Kugelmann was sneaking down that hall when the maid surprised him and precipitated the carnage."

"What do you think?" Sherlock asked.

"The public hasn't been let into the full facts. You being brother to a brother officer, I can reveal to you that the case has already been solved to most everyone's satisfaction."

"How?" Sherlock asked, a bit let down, as there would be no further mystery.

"It wasn't given out to the papers, but this morning Mary Van Winkle, a block from the pump room, ran into an officer. She was covered with blood. Which is bad."

"It couldn't be worse," Sherlock said.

"She was carrying a bloody knife. That's worse," Hubner said decisively.

"I don't see any way around the fact that she killed her husband and maid."

"Yes," Hubner responded, going on, "but I still wonder where Kugelmann was hiding during all this time. I wonder if in some oblique way he was connected to all this."

"I don't see how he could be," Sherlock had to confess.

Hubner waved his arm, as if he were directing Sherlock's

gaze down the street toward the pavilion. "As I mentioned, behind the pump room is a courtyard filled with odds and ends. Propped against the metal section of the structure is the ladder to the roof. A clue hangs there."

In front of them, through the shop window, one could see a set of parasols, set at jaunty angles, reclining on the shelf like beach umbrellas on the shale at Brighton.

"How could that provide a clue?" Sherlock queried.

The officer told him, "I visited the scene this morning. A dripping faucet has left the ground near the base of the ladder muddy. So, if you mounted the ladder and then went out on the glass above, you would leave tracks." Hubner paused, looking up reflectively while he began rubbing his shoulder. "And if I didn't pull my back working with the barbells last week ..."

"Yes?"

"I would have climbed the ladder looking for traces of the murderer's passage. And when I didn't find any, which I can't doubt would be the result of my research, this idea of him watching the Van Winkles from aloft would be shot to, to ..."

"Ribbons," Holmes offered, then he offered something else. "I propose myself as a candidate. I would be happy to climb up and look for any mud."

The sergeant contorted his face, taking it from surprise to skepticism to wariness to a statement: "That idea doesn't sound half-bad."

They left the parasols and continued their stroll. When they reached the pavilion, Hubner conferred with his fellow officers and then took Sherlock through the side entrance, where they stumbled through a long corridor and out the other side into an open space stuffed with empty cartons, cracked crockery, and gardening tools. There were a few aprons and blouses hanging on a makeshift clothesline tied over a washtub, and the door to another building hung half-open, perhaps leading to an adjacent street. The ladder stood in a wide puddle, which Sherlock gingerly forded.

He ascended systematically, methodically scanning each rung for mud samples. Having found none, he reached the roof, steadying himself on a raised stanchion to survey the glass patchwork covering the pump room. He had already detected another flaw in a public opinion that saw Kugelmann striding across the skylight to be viewed by the Van Winkles below. On one side of the oblong building's roof was a strip of tar paper roofing, covering the stock corridor below. If any intruder came up here for shelter, he or she would have hunkered down there, not out on the glass. Holmes confined his search for muddy clues to the tar paper. His long legs made stooping awkward, so it was down on his hands and knees that he studied the surface. It was hot up here, but he took his time, believing in the slow, cold scrutiny preached by Dupin.

No mud. Sherlock stood and began returning to the ladder. He glanced back and spied, about halfway across, in the gutter along the front of the roof, a slip of paper being played with by the wind.

Finally, a legitimate clue. He strode gingerly out onto the roof, testing the glass as he went, feeling quite pleased with himself, because in a sense he was living a fantasy.

Sometimes up in his bedroom, when he should have been cribbing a Latin text for an exam, he was actually reading a smuggled-in, contraband shilling dreadful featuring a star class detective like Hot Dan, Sergeant Cuff, Oily of the Yard, or one of their American cousins. This type of material took up many young men's daydreams, but few expected these stories would take a turn in their real life. So, as Sherlock crossed the glass, he felt a certain doubling of his character, following in the footsteps, as it were, of Hot Dan, whose spirit seemed to hover around him like a miasma—no, no, like an aura. He recalled Thoreau, another

American in his library, who described walking along the railroad tracks, deep in the forest, then passing into a clearing and finding light flashing reflectively from the ties below, giving him a burning halo as he left the thrown-off cloak of darkness.

Sherlock trod carefully, not allowing himself to step fully on a glass lozenge but staying on the fretwork between panes. Below him, he could see in the pump room, which was now being swept and tidied up, the floor near the tap fountains aflood with soapsuds. Two maids were scrubbing and three or four handymen tidying the front section.

He moved nervously; a few times, Sherlock felt the glass combination yield a little without cracking. He reached his target and crouched to pull free a dirty, cream-colored ticket for the upcoming Hunter's Ball. It was ripped, with part of the top torn off. On that top was the partial number _ _ _ 5. Since these tickets had been sold only over the last few days, this finding indicated whoever lost it must have been perched on this rooftop recently.

Sherlock started carefully back along the front edge of the roof, a little more confident about his footing and certainly buoyed by his discovery. There was still some "give" on the surface, but he disregarded it.

A stride too hard and his right foot snapped the brittle glasswork, and he plunged through, arms flailing, his left leg flung toward the building's front. Further panes cracked in his downward catapult. But the left leg went over the gutter and the outside wall, arresting his drop. He was through the roof only up to his waist.

People inside the building were screaming, imagining he was about to crash on top of them. Below, the soap-suds-spumed floor was sprinkled with shards of glass while Sherlock, above, half in and half out of the structure, was astride the building as if it were his horse.

Chapter 5

Cranky sat on a pallet in his jail cell, cursing the poet Baudelaire for putting him there.

He hadn't been offered any prison garb, so he still wore his checked pants, white shirt, and flamboyant if wilted yellow tie that had a peacock eye halfway up it. His checked jacket lay at his side. He was of middle height and middle weight and of a generally placid, middling temperament. His ruddy face was framed with muttonchops, setting off his regular features and black, middling eyes.

For the last four years, the good professor—he had been nicknamed Dr. Cranky by his spa associates, but his real name was Dr. Baumgarten—had been working on a long monograph on Baudelaire's chef d'oeuvre, *Les Fleurs du mal* (the evil flowers), and it had served almost as encouragement for illicit adventure. In Germany, the professor was a happily married man with three daughters. He was known to be a sober, reserved, staid Berliner. On his annual bachelor holiday, less fettered, he had begun to engage in flirtations with the maids and service girls of the various establishments. It was that which had brought him early to the pump room, where he had expected some piquant moments alone with the darling young woman, Frau Heidi, whose acquaintance he had been cultivating, but they had been rudely interrupted by the inopportune arrival of the Van Winkles. Last summer, he'd met and lost to Van Winkle at a few card parties at the resort but knew the wife only by reputation and through the banknotes she'd paid for his auctioned-off Hugo's *Les Contemplations*.

While blameless of any assault on the Van Winkles—and once the police looked at things circumspectly, he had no doubt he'd be released—he was still afraid that if things went further, his love flirtation would be exposed, something that would play havoc with his Berlin reputation and marriage. If only he hadn't been infatuated with French letters. Damn these literary decadents. How was it even possible that a respectable middle-aged man would suddenly adopt such a perverse role model?

Baudelaire, with his Creole mistress and dabblings in drugs, was no more dissolute than many another rich Frenchman. But it was his literary adventures that caught the eye. *Fleurs* was immediately banned for speaking aloud about the female version of the love that dare not speak its name. The republished, expurgated version was something of a *succès de scandale*, due, most said, to the controversy the tome had stirred up. But Cranky made out a second, unmentioned reason, hidden under the promotion of lesbian excitement.

As Cranky saw it, and noted down, *Fleurs* "pulled a fast one on the titillating darkness of high romanticism by grounding it in the everyday." Sitting in his cell, Cranky went on rehearsing his argument. Where Byron, describing himself in *Childe Harold*, wandered the continent as a "groaning loner," hinting at unspeakable, aristocratic perversions, Baudelaire "generously assumed" his readers had participated in his debaucheries beside him: At "le sein martyrisé d'une antique catin // *Nous* volons au passage un plaisir clandestine." (At the martyred breasts of the old whore // *We* take in passing a secret pleasure.) So, he speaks to his readers: *Nous*, we. We "Descend, fleuve invisible" (Go down the invisible river); we "sans horreur, à travers des ténèbres" (without any feelings of shame cross the shadows). The poet speaks to his "Hypocrite lecteur," the hypocritical reader, who wants to revel in *Les Fleurs du mal*'s filth with a look of disgust on his face but a knowing smile in his heart.

Where the English lord handled human excesses with consummate taste, something of an assurance that he saw his audience as fellow sophisticates, Baudelaire pilloried his audience as akin to "les chacals, les panthères, les lices // Les singes, les scorpions, les vautours, les serpents" (jackals, wildcats, mongrels, apes, scorpions, vultures, snakes) for whom every obscenity had to be spelled out, *not* due to his audience's innocence but *to maximize titillation*.

That was the scholarly part of his obsession, but there was also a personal side to his attraction to *Fleurs*. Under its tutelage, he was reexamining his youthful straitlacedness: neither dueling nor drinking himself under the table nor chasing landlords' daughters, he had bookwormed his way to a prominent post and classy wife. Much to be proud of, yet, perhaps much missed. So, he dabbled a little, every summer stay making the acquaintance of an accommodating young woman, and every season proceeding a little further in familiarity. This time he set his cap for Heidi, whose job was handing out glasses of water to spa patients. He had gone to the pavilion to see her as she set up for the day, when she would be unharried by thirsty guests.

Things were going as planned. He was helping the attendant up a stepladder as she adjusted a valve on the water pipe when there was the unwonted and disagreeable appearance of the Van Winkle party.

The front-runner in the door was the sour old Henry Van Winkle, with his wife, Mary, and her lady's maid, Molly, following behind. The Wall Street buccaneer was in Karlsbad every August, and last year Cranky had crossed arms more than once with him at the baccarat table in the local casino. He owed the millionaire a small sum, which was, to his mind, so tiny it might be considered a debt of honor rather than a financial matter. Still, he had been remitting him money by mail, even having to sell books to do so, but hadn't paid the whole amount back yet. So, his was a particularly unwelcome appearance at just this crucial instant.

The old blunderbuss, who couldn't remember people's names but, it was said, never forgot a number, called out as he entered the pump room. "Well, Farebrother, you old dog, take your hands out of nursie's petticoats." Then came the grating laugh: "Aha-ha."

Van Winkle was coatless, hatless, and bedecked in a ruffled gambler's shirt and striped pants. His face was a study in contrasts: well-trimmed, curlicued mustache versus a wild, uncombed white beard; weak mouth and button nose versus coal-black, incandescent eyes.

"I assure you, sir—" Cranky replied to him, dropping his arms so quickly Heidi was thrown off balance and fell from the third step into his arms.

"Ah, even better, you old crow. Didn't know you had it in you," the millionaire said, letting out his ugly laugh.

As Cranky looked for words, the color went up Heidi's cheeks like pheasants flushing up from the underbrush.

Van Winkle interrupted him not saying anything. "None of your excuses, Billie. We're all gentlemen here." He laughingly addressed the attendant. "Serve me up a half-liter bumper of your punch there, hussy. Snap to it."

The water, after the faucet adjustment, had already started flowing into the large basin beneath the jets, which was kept full due to the lovely shimmering effect it produced, sending reflections rippling off the glass walls.

Now Cranky found speech. "Sir, I resent your tone."

"Excuse me, Herr Winkle," the girl broke in, moving into a stumbling English, "but we are disallowed to server the restorative beverage—"

She didn't get any further. "And do you disallow my boot up your backside?" he replied. Before Cranky could leap to the girl's defense, Van Winkle stepped up to Heidi and proffered a small bill. "Forgive my testy outburst." He pressed the money into her hand, which did nothing to repel it. "Perhaps we could bend our dear regulations this one time."

"I can give you a liter glass, a big one, half filled up. We don't seem to have any half liters here."

"That's not doctor's orders, is it?"

"We have more in the storage across the street. I will just nip across if you'd like."

"Of course *I'd like*," Van Winkle parroted in an offensive imitation of Heidi's endearing but mincing tone. "Go to it, wench." Then he clapped his hands in the air to accelerate her progress, as if she were a performing horse.

Cranky stepped with her to the door of the pavilion, saying in a lowered tone, "You don't have to accept his insolence," as he eyed the crumpled bill in her hand, which was larger than any of the little cash presents he had given her the past few days.

"Don't trouble yourself. We have to deal with all kinds of guests."

"At least let me accompany you across the street," he said, opening the door.

"Why thank you, Rudolph," Heidi said with a flirtatious smile.

He was thrilled. It was the first time she had used his given name. His elation was short-lived as it was immediately broken by a summons from the American.

"Fairskin, I need your help. Don't stop up your ears. Come over here."

Inopportunely, Cranky remembered his debt of honor, which he had unfortunately stopped remitting due to unexpected household expenses. He was four months in arrears.

"I'll be right after, Heidi," he called as he turned back to the American party.

"I might need a little assistance in this project. Nobody

likes my idea, these women. But I think you can understand me. I confess that only now do I see your colors, old Fairskin. I knew you last year for a gamester, yes, but also one with a solid head, a quick grasp, a scholar with deep eyes. Yes, siree, like the gray eyes of the Owl of Minerva, flies at dawn, they say. Lo and behold, now I find you are also a gallant of the old school. Quick to the attack."

Cranky blinked, slowly like the mentioned bird. How many of these strokes of Van Winkle's had been dipped in irony, it was hard to tell.

"What exactly is your controversial project?" Cranky interrupted.

"Straight to the heart of the matter. I like that. And I saw you in action. Apologies. I think I interrupted you right when you were closing the deal. Couldn't be helped. I can see you don't blame me for what can't be avoided. No spite." The millionaire let his voice drop an octave. "Not spitting like one of these wildcats here." His elbow indicated the two women, who were laying towels out on one of the benches.

The millionaire moved in closer to talk more privately. "My wife's loose in the hilts. I'd like to make her into a tar candle. If I could catch her with that fancy-pants riding instructor Von Pelt. You know how they make a tar candle?"

The women came forward. Mary was wearing a stylish walking dress and an imperious frown. Her dress was a pleasant dun color with wavy dark lines placed at the neck and midriff and on a bottom ruffle. The lines were also on the sleeve cuffs so that when her arms hung loose at her sides, they continued the line on the garment.

Her face was pretty, containing a pert nose and full mouth. Her ice-blue eyes expressed eternal skepticism.

The Black maid, Molly, could be counterpointed to Heidi, the bath attendant: Heidi tall where Molly was short, Molly dark skinned where Heidi had a complexion like a snowdrift, and Molly's cropped, kinky hair on display while

Heidi's blond thatch was squeezed down by a sort of tam-o'-shanter. Molly's uniform consisted of a blue blouse covered by a white smock that puffed out along the bottom. Heidi's uniform had a black blouse with a white covering apron, V-crossed at the top, and full skirt. Heidi had a jolly, care-free look with soft features and purple-gray eyes. Molly was warier; her dark lips and dark eyes wore a stern, sad look with a touch of the haughtiness of Mary.

Van Winkle turned to the fountain and began paddling with his hands in the basin beneath the jets. "This water is the purest in the place," he said, still ruffling the surface so some slopped on the floor. Cranky had to step back to avoid getting splashed.

"Say, juggler," Van Winkle said, turning to the maid, "bring me that heavy towel to put around my back." As Molly turned, Van Winkle smacked his lips, "Superb curve to her bust, wouldn't you say?"

Doesn't seem to have much concern for his wife, Cranky thought as the maid returned with the swathing, which Van Winkle put around his shoulders as he began unbuttoning his shirt.

Cranky was confused and set off. "What are you up to, sir? This is no gymnasium."

Van Winkle indicated the waterspouts with a head slash. "I'm of the opinion that this drinking water is the only liquid worth its salt in this establishment. Not that it has salt in it." He smiled at his own witticism. "The kind of stuff they give us to bathe in. Phew. It's polluted with creosote. A slough."

"What is that to me?" Cranky asked.

"Well, I thought I'd soak my backside in this fountain. It's not deep enough for a full bath, but I'll just settle in a minute. I've got my soap, haven't I?"

The wife showed it to him, a square bar.

"And my towels?"

The maid displayed an armful.

"Help me climb up, Fairchild," Van Winkle said to the professor.

"People drink this water," the good Cranky objected.

"I'm a millionaire. My skin is sacred. People would pay to drink this water after I washed up in it. Stand in line, they would."

Cranky was taken aback by this whole procedure. "I can't let this happen."

"Don't worry, I'll give you the first glassful. Aha-ha. So, if you can't boost me up, make yourself useful. Go across the street and stand by the door and warn off Frau Dussell. Wouldn't want to give her the shock of her life."

Damnée, if the man hadn't given the maid his shirt and was on the verge of taking down his trousers.

Cranky sputtered, "I'll do nothing of the sort. This is outrageous."

Van Winkle cut him short. "You know, Cranky, I allow you here on sufferance. You owe me a nice sum, which I forbore dunning after your piddling excuses. I disdained even answering your letters. Bigger fish. But if you cross me ..."

"This is like blackmail."

Not a laugh but a "Hrmp" from Van Winkle. "Call it what you like." He went back to stripping his trousers. "I could haul you down to court. Even Germany has laws for welchers."

"I will repay—"

"No more dilly-dallying. Get to your post, roisterer."

Badly chastened, Cranky exited the scene of humiliation quickly and crossed the street, hurrying to head Heidi off in the storage facility.

As he stepped through the door, he stopped short. A savage hyena, escaped from the zoo, was crouched behind one of the boxes that filled the space and was preparing to pounce. Or so it seemed. Closer inspection revealed to him he was looking at a very realistic animal mask, protruding from an open box of masquerade animal masks.

Heidi was calling him from upstairs. "Please, I need your assistance." She seemed almost frightened. He squeezed through the cartons packing the lower room to reach a ladder, which he climbed as quickly as he could.

The second floor was as stuffed with boxes as the first, but in more disorder. There was broken, dust-covered glass on the floor. Heidi stood in the front, trying to lift the window. "Please, Rudolph, the window is stuck. We must open it. I can't breathe in this dust."

He hurried to her side and, with some straining, threw up the sash. For a moment, he was transfixed as he saw the wife, Mary, exit the pavilion. He watched to see where she was going when there was a scream from inside the pump room. Mary turned around and rushed back.

"What's going on?" Heidi asked.

"Something's up, but I—"

"What's wrong?"

He told her, "I'm stuck in the frame here. Could you be so good as to give me a heave?"

Once he was disentangled, Cranky hurried as fast as he could down the steps. Heidi stayed behind. Once on the street, he crossed to the pavilion and got another fright. Inside, a wolf-man, or rather, a wolf-masked man, was standing over two bloody bodies.

Not waiting for the man to see him, Cranky took to his heels, which now appeared to be winged like Mercury's.

That was his story to the police.

∾

It seemed to him that he wouldn't be in jail long. Heidi would vouch for him. Besides, his trifling gambling debt to Van Winkle was hardly enough to warrant him committing a bold-stroke murder. That didn't bother him. What was problematic was the possibility that the press had caught wind of his gambling IOUs and his dalliance. That could cause havoc with his reputation. What of his teaching job at a religious college, his wife and three daughters? Better not to anticipate trouble. As St. Matthew put it, "Sufficient to the day is the evil thereof. Take, therefore, no thought of the morrow."

He rocked back on his bunk, balancing that quote with a more melancholy one: "Enlève-moi frégate! // Loin! Loin! Ici la boue est faite de nos pleurs!" (Ocean liner, transport me far, far away! Here even the mud in the streets is soaked with tears.)

The jailer disturbed these gloomy meditations by bringing a visitor to his cell. It was Dr. Arbuthnot, companion of many a jolly evening, now coming to share his time of sorrow. Cranky slid over and Arbuthnot joined him on his cot, so they resembled nothing so much as two thickly bearded pensioners sunning on a park bench in the Tiergarten, except that the only sun was a thin, bifurcating line on the wall resembling the tracing of a willow branch.

There were only two cells in the small building, and Cranky's the only one with a tenant. Van Winkle's wife must have been lodged elsewhere. The tiny cage was barely furnished; a cot and a pail in a postage stamp lined with sooty gray stone. The guard room also had only one occupant, a policeman who had been lounging in the door when Arbuthnot arrived. Glancing out, Arbuthnot noted the guard seemed to have absented himself totally.

Sitting down, the visitor asserted he had come only to commiserate, not to get an inside track on the scandal; still, as Cranky could only occupy his thoughts by running over the morning's events, he retold his story, this time taking a less sanguine view. He ended lamenting, "Mary Van Winkle must know I owed her husband money. She's probably telling the police that I wanted her husband dead because that gambling debt put me in his power."

"But, *lieber Freund*, you have Heidi to back up your story," Arbuthnot reassured him.

"Unless the police decide the two of us were in collusion. It's as if I were collaborating on my own death sentence."

"How do you see that?" Arbuthnot asked.

"I told them I saw Mary enter the pavilion after the scream. That means she didn't commit the first murder."

"Established. But that also exonerates you, as you were in the storage room when the crime took place," Arbuthnot mentioned as he stood up and paced over to the branch's light, allowing it to fall partly on the shoulder of his topcoat.

"That's my story," Cranky said, "but this devil Hubner, who is heading the investigation, proposed a more sinister line of action when he questioned me. He wondered if I were not frantic to cancel my debt before my family found out about it. The only way I could do so was by eliminating my creditor.

"So, Hubner speculated, I somehow suborned Fräulein Dussell to help me with this treachery. When I first exited the pump room, rather than crossing the street, I backtracked to the door that led to the corridor behind the pavilion. I peeped out, waiting on my chance, which, Hubner said, I knew might not come. I saw Mary exit and then Molly came back and surprised me, so I cut her down. However, I lost control of the situation because as Molly cried out and stumbled from the room and as I was about to attack the half-undressed millionaire, his wife returned. Then my luck turned again. Mary ran back out and it was the work of a moment to kill the loudmouthed but physically weak Van Winkle.

"Work accomplished, I went into the storeroom building for the first time, handed Heidi the bloody smock I had donned to go on my killing spree, and ran prattling to the police."

"Outrageous," Arbuthnot replied, and he paced the small space as if he were measuring its dimensions. "What a dummkopf this Hubner is. Instead of going into this rigmarole of plot and counterplot, why not adopt the simplest solution. The half-cracked millionaire kills the maid for an unknown reason, his wife comes in, sees his deed, wrestles the knife away from him, and strikes out."

"But, dear friend, you are missing what I mentioned to you."

"What's that?" Arbuthnot asked, halting his walk.

"I saw a masked man in the room."

Arbuthnot, back to pacing, turned away from the cot and said, over his shoulder, "Yes, you did say that. That adds to the puzzle. Who else would be wandering around that early?"

"Yes, it does add a new factor. There are so many possibilities," Cranky replied, not expressing his full thoughts, which ran deeper. After all, he thought, how well did he know this Arbuthnot, whom he'd come across this morning as he was taking his stroll to the pavilion? Moreover, he went on considering, more than once Arbuthnot had spoken angrily and intemperately of this class of buccaneers of finance in general and of Van Winkle in particular.

The willow branch of light was lifting slowly up the wall, falling on Arbuthnot's back and shoulders as he passed, making it seem as if he were wandering the woods. He offered a new line of thought, which made Cranky, at least temporarily, dismiss Arbuthnot as a suspect.

Arbuthnot said, "What about Kugelmann? He was concealed in the vicinity and had nothing to lose." He stopped talking and walking, brushing his forehead as if trying to clear off the lines of light that were coming into his eyes because of where he had chosen to stand.

Cranky had another deep thought, which he voiced. "If Kugelmann had nothing to lose, why would he put on an animal head?"

He didn't voice the second part of that idea. The mask would only be used by someone who had to conceal his identity from those who knew him and were on the scene. For example, Cranky's bottle companion, Arbuthnot, who was nervously striding about right in front of him. Cranky watched Arbuthnot a moment.

As the cell was so narrow, his friend was going through a checked dance: stride forward, pull up short, turn around, another stride, another abrupt halt.

And at just that moment, as if blocked by a cloud, the willow blinked out.

Chapter 6

Eleanor lay across the bed like a swath of tulle.

She was considering which letter to mail, or, rather, as it was getting a little late to send it off, which letter to hand Lissagaray when first she saw him.

She was inclining toward the first, the complete severing of their connection. She should rip up the other one.

Her betrothed, Lissagaray had accepted her as she truly was, but the problem was that she didn't want to be that way. She didn't want to move, as she was, from being her father's amanuensis on articles for the *New York Tribune* to Lissagaray's for *The History of the Commune*. Sure, she was proud of her work. How many women her age were writing articles in French and Spanish concerning the political situations in those respective nations or giving speeches at workingmen's conventions? But the articles were commissioned, the speeches booked by her father. For all these years, her father had treated her as a ... goose. She was getting old enough at twenty to see this no longer suited. The letter to her fiancé, once she gave it to him, would open her independent life.

She raised herself carefully from the bed, trying not to dent her bustle.

Eleanor bowed to convention in wearing a bustle, but she refused to add the refinement of decorations others adopted. Many women adorned themselves with ornaments: multiple flounces, velvet bands, bows, rainbow beads, tinsel, paste jewels, ruchings (pleats), braids, feathers, and passementeries (French lace)—for Sherlock's mother, flowers—so the woman ended up looking like a pawnshop window.

When Eleanor collapsed on the bed, she had to take care to fall at a certain angle. She was dressed in a Princess Polonaise day dress with cream bodice and overskirt. The skirt looped at the sides and gathered to a small bustle at the back. So, if she had lain on her back, the bustle, aside from being damaged, would have turned her to either side. If she collapsed to one or the other side, the bustle still would be shaken out of place. So, she lay down flat face, her nose pressing into the spread as if she were a girl sheltering in her mother's skirts.

Now she carefully lifted up and went to the desk, picked up the second, temporizing letter, and made ready to shred it.

There was a tap at the door, and in a minute the chambermaid tramped in. It was Yvette, a sulky-looking woman. Where Swandra was pert and vivacious, Yvette was a quiet pool, a dark study. She was quick, always moving, always active, her brown eyes flicking back and forth. She was petite, barely filling out the same maid uniform Swandra seemed to be pushing through. She had a small, sharp nose and delicate mouth.

Eleanor classified maids as hard shell or soft shell. While the hard-shelled ones took more coaxing, once you broke them open, they were as loaded with hotel gossip as the soft ones.

"Can I tidy the bed, mam'selle?" Yvette inquired.

"Please do. Thank you," Eleanor said over her shoulder.

She again lifted the folded-over second letter, but where her hands should have been giving it a strong tug, it seemed as if her finger was exerting its own will and merely tapped the paper along the corner.

"*C'est fini*," Yvette said.

Turning all the way around in her seat to thank her full

face, which was only polite, Eleanor saw her scribbling. "What are you writing?" she asked, switching to French.

"Just a note to myself," she said, turning the pad to face Eleanor, who made out what looked like hieroglyphics or the Chinese she had invented as a child.

"Is that shorthand?"

"It's my own invention. I just put down the room number and draw a little candle. That's to tell me to stock a candle here later."

"You …" Eleanor trailed off, not wanting to embarrass the girl.

"I never learned to write. In my town, the priest charged three sous for school."

"This was in France?" Eleanor said, turning her chair completely around.

"Once France, Alsace." Germany had seized that French province after the 1871 war. "Eventually, I moved to Paris."

The two switched to German.

"Yvette, I just wondered if you've heard anything about those horrible crimes?"

"The wife must have done it. It was shown at the picnic. She was falling for Von Pelt. She only married that moneybags because he was rich. What the English call 'a marriage of inconvenience.' I heard she came into quite a large fortune after the war. Her husband, brother, and father died fighting for the Confederacy. Once she was of age, she gambled it all up. That's when she went husband hunting and, I heard, the richer the better. She had no real feeling for her spouse. What's the opposite of love birds?"

"Hate birds, I guess," Eleanor contributed, then turned direction. "Let's get back to the picnic you mentioned."

Yvette was leaning forward as if she were about to topple over. Eleanor was sitting in a chair right beside the bed, looking at her across the tightly cosseted sheet and spread as if they stood on opposite sides of a streamlet.

"Why don't you sit?" Eleanor offered, and Yvette sank onto the bed.

"The maid who was with them described it so well to me, I could almost see it," she said. "Von Pelt was riding past and he stopped to talk, staying in the saddle. He mentioned his horse was Spirit."

"A spirited horse?" Eleanor asked.

"No, named Spirit," the maid said. "But he was a charger. He had ridden it to war against France."

"I see."

Eleanor, who knew all the principals, could also visualize what happened. It probably took place in the meadow near the red three-kilometer road marker. She had visited it once.

～

The space was incongruous, a huge, natural glade surrounded by a thick, tangled forest that from a distance seemed impenetrable. It was like a calm tract of sea ringed by churning waves. The trees were so closely pressed together, they seemed conspiratorial, whispering among themselves like the greenhouse plants in Hoffmann's "The Golden Flower Pot." There was a carpet of fluffy grass, here and there pressed down by previous holiday makers and not yet sprung back up, as if it took a while for pleasant memories to fade.

The hotel maids spread out a large blue checked tablecloth on the sward and unpacked a hamper filled with cheese, cuts of meat, and slices of pumpernickel. The Black maid, Molly, as Eleanor visualized it, was uncorking a bottle of white wine when Von Pelt came riding his beautiful roan horse out of the dark glade.

He made some saucy remarks, then Mary walked up to stroke the horse, which shied away.

"Stand back, my lady," he said courteously. "Spirit is a fractious beast."

"You seem to have firm control of her," Mary remarked.

He politely got down from the horse so they could speak on a level. "I know this animal well, so I can work her, but she would never let anyone else sit her."

Mary laughed. "I think I could keep her in line. I've been riding since I was ten years old. If you don't know the thoroughbreds of the old South, you don't know bad-tempered steeds."

"It's not her temper. She just doesn't like strangers."

Mary took another tack. "I heard you're a betting man. I spied you through the window of the casino with that card-sharper Pricklestone."

For some reason, Von Pelt began to look uneasy. "I just look on. I don't play."

Mary prodded him. "I think I could master her."

Unexpectedly, according to Yvette, Von Pelt acceded.

"If I can ride her to that big Scots pine and back, you owe me a riding lesson. I'm already an expert, but there are a few points on which I might improve my horsemanship."

"And if you lose?" was Von Pelt's rejoinder.

Before she could answer, her maid, Molly, ran forward. "Begging your ladyship's pardon, but you're taking this jesting much too far. This mare is madness incarnate. It's like the four horsemen in the Bible riding to bring a world of perdition on us. You get on her, you are bound to break your sweet neck."

For the first time, Mary showed a flaring of real emotion, saying to Molly, "You don't order me about. Stay in your place." Turning to Von Pelt, she shifted to teasing. "If I can't handle her and you win, I will grant you a kiss."

With that, she snatched the reins from his gloved hands and was mounted and flying across the meadow. She rode back in a more leisurely fashion and dismounted with a flourish.

"So, there was no kiss," Eleanor said after Yvette had finished the story.

"Ah, but there was a flying kiss added."

"What's this?"

"A hand-blown kiss as he rode off," Yvette said, smiling to herself.

"You describe everything so well I can almost see it."

"That's what I said to my friend the maid. She acted all the parts," Yvette said, closing her little book. "But I must be going," she added, sitting stock-still on the bed.

She expected Eleanor to rise first, which she did, going to the table and dipping into her sachet for a small coin. She went back and handed it to the hard shell, who now was standing and reaching over the maid-made bed to accept the gratuity.

After Yvette departed, Eleanor sat back down at her table and put her hands forcefully on the corners of the second letter, but she paused, trying to remember where she had heard the name Pricklestone, which Yvette had mentioned. Now she had it. It was something she had overheard at the Pembroke soiree two nights past.

Eleanor had been trapped into talking to a couple of made-up dullards, both ranking officers, one Austrian, one German, whose topic was war. The discussion was not of tactics, so-called *Kunst des Krieges*, but on whether a unified realm, something new in Germany, which had been united by Prussia after the war with France, could field a better army than a multinational, dual nation like the one of Austria-Hungary. Its doubled name indicated its structure: two kings, two legislatures, two souls.

Normally, such a conversation would not go on in front of a lady, who was thought uninterested in such worldly topics, but finding from her comments that she was a well-read, well-versed bluestocking, they let themselves get carried away.

Directly behind her, Pembroke and Smallweed were chatting about the then-living Van Winkle, his marriage and fortune.

They were waiting in the drawing room for the door to open, which would let them in for a cold buffet.

Pembroke's suite was top crust: two bedrooms, living space, bath, and dining room. Eleanor recognized the rooms were decorated in the late Biedermeier style. To her, the form represented a veiled attempt at national reconciliation, in that while Austria and France were at daggers drawn politically, the Austrian middle class had opted for furniture that was modeled on and simplified the classically uncomplicated lines of the designs of Napoleonic France.

As the style aged, more and more fussy German ornament was added, like barnacles accumulating on a ship's bottom. In the living room where they waited was a table whose chairs had the typical airy back made of two symmetrical leaf patterns, but where earlier these would have been plain, now at the top of the ovals were little cherrywood butterflies. There was a beautiful, sinuous small sofa with the style's barely inflated cushions and discreet patterned upholstery but with a wooden fringe of floral flower heads just daring to peek out along the bottom of the seat. Most characteristic was a walnut display case, lightly assembled but solid, holding trays of shepherdess figurines, watched over by their swains as they stood among their woolly flocks.

As she glanced around, she kept expecting the doors to open, and so she didn't break off from her group as it was about to dissolve anyway with the stampede to the dinner, but she did overhear a tantalizing smidgen from widow Smallweed during a lull in the military windbags' blather.

One of her military acquaintances, the Austrian, had been intoning about "the grand war" with France, not the petty, two-manned conflict Prussia had lately won, but the battle against Napoleon in his first eastward advance, which wielded together Prussia, lower Germany, Austria-Hungary, and Russia, with all "these armies all carefully orchestrated to divide the field and the defense."

"I'm afraid you've picked your example from thin air, a very thin, upper-Alpine air," the German rebutted. "For what results did your 'orchestrated' minions achieve? Disaster and capitulation in the face of a unified, national force."

"True, both our nations were stymied by the French foe, but I believe we learned and learned well from those defeats."

"It was a stain on our honor," the German suggested, "one I readily admit, especially now that we have repaid the favor by trouncing the good Napoleon's nephew at Sedan."

As they both considered that, Eleanor managed to listen in to what Smallweed was saying. It was concerning an incident, a contretemps between Van Winkle and his wife in a fight in the lobby of Ludwig's.

Smallweed stated, "You left too early, m'dear. I heard from—oh, what's the name of that little chit of a girl with red hair? I call her Sagittarius, the archer, 'cause of her eyebrows. She said after most of the dining hall had been cleared, about four or five young people were still standing there, immobile in their places as if fixed by the stare of a basilisk."

Pembroke prodded her. "You said they set up a theater?"

"Not so formal, but one young lady had come tail end and missed the excitement, so these wags—one miss and two young sparks—took their places, standing for the couple and Von Pelt, and did a reenactment. It seemed history repeated itself with a new premise. Now everyone in the scene was either a fashionable young blade or a lovely belle, not a dried-up mummy or female centaur or a cashiered mountebank."

Pembroke asked further, "So who took the part of Von Pelt?"

"It was that character Pricklestone, a delightful gentleman, full of fun, and quite a mimic."

There was something suspicious about that gent, Eleanor thought. He stayed in the same hotel they did, so she had glimpsed him in passing. Always dressed nattily in conservative grays. Not flashily styled, but still distinctly tasteful. She remembered him in dark trousers, a thigh-length gray coat, and white shirt, and around his neck, not a tie, rather a kind of very light, short muffler, bunched up so as to hide half his face.

For all his debonair air, there was something sinister about him. Moreover, come to think of it, more than once she had seen him on the fringe of the Van Winkle entourage, not part of it but trailing along. There was something in his eyes that one might see in a fox glancing furtively through a fence at a plump hen.

She put all of that out of her mind, as it was time for a walk with Father.

Chapter 7

Going to meet Eleanor, Arbuthnot was proceeding along a railing-girded set of stairs, taking his early-evening constitutional, a half-bent, unlit stogie protruding from his mouth as he vigorously worked his ashplant. Dr. Feckles had told him to cut out smoking but could hardly forbid his nursing a cigar between his teeth. He wanted to see Eleanor to discuss family matters.

Ostensibly they were going to chat about her work on the Paris Commune book, but Arbuthnot planned to discreetly—as much as he could be discreet—probe her relations to this unsuitable potential son-in-law with whom she was working on the book.

When she arrived wearing the same cream blouse she had on nearly every day and carrying a blue, hotel-provided parasol, which she must have grabbed from one of the elephant-foot containers, they walked into a small park and stopped at a bench. Arbuthnot sat, resting the cane in the crook of his arms and lolling back while she stood before him.

In Arbuthnot's estimation, Karlsbad parks were adverse to offering shade. They had an ample supply of bushy trees, but they were always set well back from the paths, separated from them by an expanse of greensward. The only object near enough to the benches to offer shadow cover were the plentiful statues. Perhaps the city fathers were afraid of them tipping off their plinths, since all the stone men stood ramrod straight, making no extravagant gestures nor riding any top-heavy stallions.

Under a sliver of shade offered by a famous states-man, Arbuthnot praised his daughter for her work on the Commune book. "We can't allow this history to be silenced," he said.

Eleanor said wearily, "The Commune was strangled in the cradle like the serpents Hercules choked when he was in swaddling clothes. Lissagaray estimates twenty thousand Communards were killed outright, scores sent to prisons and devil's islands."

Arbuthnot nodded. "It makes your blood boil."

To keep their blood from literally boiling on this fiery day, Eleanor positioned herself so her sunshade gave them both a larger portion of shadow.

She continued, "And to add to the outrage, the Communards, hounded out of the country or killed, are held up as a threat to justify the repressions of every dark regime in Europe, our own place of exile not excluded."

Arbuthnot was staring at the ramrod statue looming over them. "You know, since I wrote that masterful pamphlet defending the uprising, I've had to reassess or at least reshuffle some of my opinions about government."

"How so, *Pater*?"

Arbuthnot fanned himself with a newspaper he was carrying. "I thought the worker would come to power just as the middle class did after the French Revolution. Just as the bourgeoisie did, the workers would simply replace the state personnel who had been serving the king, telling the new functionaries to about-face and work for them. I thought the conquering workers would simply file into the chambers of state and take their seats."

"Isn't that what happened?" Eleanor asked.

Arbuthnot was using a red handkerchief, not unlike the one Kugelmann had worn, to mop his brow. "Yes and no. They took the seats, but they had to move them around to make the government more democratic. Item: every representative was subject to immediate recall if he violated the electors' will. Item: all jobs rotated, so you couldn't occupy your high seat for long. Item: all pay was equalized, so every clerk at the post office, every judge, every street sweeper collected the same."

"Yes," she jumped in, "you've talked of this before. But Lissagaray said—"

"Let me stop you midsentence. You always oppose Lissagaray's opinion to mine."

She replied, "And you don't like it. One can be sure about that."

Inadvertently, she tilted the parasol away so Arbuthnot was half-blinded by the sun's glare. "That's not what concerns me," he asserted. "I'd rather hear your own opinions, which are fully as informed as his. You defer to this mountebank."

Eleanor came back, "He was in the thick of the fighting. He's no poser."

"Oh yes," Arbuthnot said, "I grant you that, and I brought this wolf indoors." He quoted from Othello's speech where the Moor describes how the father introduced him to the daughter:

Her father loved me; oft invited me;
Still question'd me the story of my life,
From year to year, the battles, sieges, fortunes,
That I have passed.... This to hear
Would Desdemona seriously incline.

Arbuthnot was happy with his tag of Shakespeare but regretted employing the word "mountebank," an untrue thrust. To soften his statements, he went on, "The man has done great service for the cause. His book will go crashing against all the lies and doggerel that has come out in the hired press. But, I think, he is not so good for you, Tussy. He is too demanding, always puts himself first, always—"

Eleanor said, "Are you describing Lissagaray or yourself?"

Arbuthnot coughed and swallowed some pride, not wanting her rudeness to stop him from delivering his opinion with some prudence. He asked, "Could you move your parasol over a notch? I'm in the sun."

She did so, though it seemed as if the fire in her eyes was casting as much glare as the sun.

Arbuthnot embroidered on what he'd been saying. "I'm only thinking of your own good, Empress. I know I've overtaxed you, but you are not married to your family. Once you find a good mate, you will move away as Laura and Jenny have. Of course, they both keep up the struggle, even with their children. And they have good husbands. That's why I worry about your choice."

He had more to say, but she undercut the whole basis of his argument by saying, "Dear Mohr, I already wrote him a letter breaking our engagement."

"*Wunderbar.*"

She clarified, "Well, not quite that. I wrote him one letter calling off our relation and another where I say we should taper it off. I'm not sure which to mail."

"Here, help me up," Arbuthnot requested. He was ready to resume his saunter, letting her go back to the hotel.

Before sending her off, he said, "If you want to swell your father's heart, go straight to your room, tear the temporizing letter in two, and special-post the breakoff letter. I'll pay the cost."

They parted, and with no umbrella to protect him, Arbuthnot decided to walk down to the river's edge, where there was likely to be more shade and a favorable breeze, freshened along the water.

Having unexpectedly and happily resolved the problem of her daughter's fiancé, which had troubled him on sleepless nights, he felt another worry replace that irritating bother. This was the young Sherlock.

The youth had a fine mind, though he was overattached to adventure yarns. That was where the problem lay. Sherlock was always looking for hidden passages and masqueraded identities. Although he and Tussy were only staying a few more days, it would be damnably inconvenient if the boy uncovered his true identity and got the authorities wrought up.

Not only had Sherlock shown them the Poe story, a relatively mild, thoughtful piece, but Arbuthnot suspected he read penny dreadfuls. Being an indulgent father for once, he hadn't upbraided his girls when he found they had concealed a collection of pulp reading, such as *Helen Trueblood, Girl Detective*, and *Oily of the Yard*. He let them keep their trove but at the time couldn't help himself from an impromptu lecture.

As good socialists, he told them, it was a bit hypocritical to read such stories, which were so heavy with whitewash. Hadn't they heard about the strikes in America? If the culprits were the capitalists, their ready tools were the detectives of the Pinkerton agency and Phelps-Dodge, who served as infiltrators, instigators, and union busters. None of this history was told to the adolescent readers of *Sergeant Cuff* and such balderdash.

Sherlock, Arbuthnot imagined, devoured this fare. As a proud member of the Squirearchy, the youth was likely ignorant of US labor troubles; although, as a bighearted fellow, he would probably side with the aggrieved toilers if he knew all the facts. At the moment, what concerned Arbuthnot was Sherlock's tiresomely inquisitive nature.

It was hardly Arbuthnot's imagination that at dinner last night he'd caught stray side glances from Sherlock, looks akin to those a cat tosses when sidling past a caged canary.

Arbuthnot was considering this when he made his way down a pillar of stairs, going toward the River Teplá. The most pleasant walk in this still, hot day was along the stream. He was just coming to the watercourse when he ran into Dr. Feckles mopping his brow, hurrying in the same direction Arbuthnot was traveling.

Feckles was a mousy-looking man with an indecisive expression that disappeared as soon as he launched into one of his favorite topics. Then his lackluster brown eyes and infirm, tentative mouth became sparkling and animated. He also hid a sheen of physical weakness under elegant furnishings. He wore a top hat and a knee-length brown coat over a gray vest buttoned all the way up, topped by a prominent white collar.

"Good doctor," Feckles said in greeting as Arbuthnot descended the last stairs to the river platform, "I owe you an expression of thanks for protecting my wife this morning."

"It was nothing. The man was tired and weakened. God knows what he was doing there."

"On the side of the building?" Feckles asked.

"No, in the city itself, dodging from zoo to belfry to pump room. We are in the mountains, after all. He could have climbed through the forests as easily, more easily than climbing your chimney."

"Yes, but there's a psychological rightness to it."

"You say?"

Feckles paused them in the stroll along the water and pointed ahead to the Lázeňská Bridge. "Have you ever noticed everyone cocks their heads as they pass that bridge?"

"Can't say I did."

"That's the bridge where the Duchess Colloredo-Mannsfeld was mowed down by the assassin's bullet. They say her noble blood is coursing in the water. She tumbled out of her seat and onto the parapet, tried to rise, and died astraddle as if the bridge were her mare."

"And you conclude?"

"It's a scientific principle that the murderer is drawn back to the scene of the crime."

They both stood staring at the structure, which, in fact, was not much to look at. The river was narrow enough so that the span was only four or five carriage lengths across, with all of them moving to the gentlemen's side of the river in a one-way progress. They both gazed as intently as if some other crime, perhaps a robbery, would soon take place.

"Scientific, you say," Arbuthnot commented.

"One needs to know *Naturphilosophie*, as defined by Dr. Lorenz Oken."

"I see."

"All things—human, mechanical, mineral—are connected by a spirit, not in a mystical sense, but through energy. If a violent retribution, say, occurs at a crossroads, then the land, the streets, become overlaid with a dark, electric aura. The place becomes something of a lodestone."

"How is that?"

"It now has negative magnetism. At the same time, those enveloped by the first wave of violence are 'tinctured' with an opposed, positive charge, and, most naturally, the killer receives the strongest influx of this energy. So, his positive polarity is drawn inexorably toward the magnetic center. Q.E.D., Kugelmann had to stay in town due to these impulses."

While Arbuthnot, in his heart, took this "science" to be little more than organized insanity made up by dummkopfs, their two-man sightseeing—both had accompanied the discussion with covert glances at the bridge—did seem to confirm the existence of the attention-holding power of the scene of bloodshed, given that Sergeant Hubner had signaled to them in passing and both Arbuthnot and Feckles had remained oblivious, staring at the span until the officer stepped directly into their line of sight, saying, "Why, Dr. Feckles, just the man I hoped to spot."

"Really," Feckles replied, airily. "I'm not that hard to find."

"I couldn't find you this morning," Hubner commented,

not budging from his place on the sidewalk, so everyone had to dodge around him.

"I was at the hotel clinic," Feckles said.

"And last night, where were you then?"

"Impertinent question."

"Not at all. Your wife said you got in quite late."

"As you know, Sergeant Hubner, the Freudenbergs have a manor a few miles deep in the forest—plenty of money, plenty of liver complaints, both father and son. When I go to wait on them, I'm often kept late and have to either bed down at their fortress or ride in when everyone is asleep."

"Good doctor, I am not questioning your nocturnal habits," the policeman said, slightly flinching as a passing maid almost poked him with her parasol. "I am just wondering, seeing as you were walking the streets quite late, whether you saw anything unusual near the pump room, like someone reconnoitering the building."

"I'm sorry, Officer, but I was bone weary, and after stabling my horse at the stroke of midnight, I could do no more than put one foot in front of the other. I didn't notice anything." The doctor paused and then went on, "If that's all your questions, I have things to do at home."

Hubner nodded acquiescence, and as Feckles turned to go, Arbuthnot made to accompany the doctor, as he had one question to the man in his medical capacity. Hubner fell in step beside them, saying, "That bridge is a symbol of tragic love."

"Good sergeant," Arbuthnot objected, "are you one of those sentimental dummkopfs that think this was a crime of passion?"

Unperturbed, Hubner explained, "I have made a thorough research of the Serbian Independence movement and learned that Kugelmann was a reformer, not an anarchist. Although there is some counterevidence, I still see the murder as one of pure fealty to love. If you know *Werther*, and no good German or Austrian should be without a copy, you'll see how a red-hot, fiery love can suddenly turn to ice when the lover is spurned.

"Goethe, our national treasure. I put his picture on my wall in the place of first prominence."

He ended his peroration with, "I think murders for love are the only poetic crimes." Then he pointed to the bridge. "Why don't I show you exactly what took place."

"Were you an eyewitness?" Feckles asked with eagerness.

"I wasn't on the spot but patrolling near at hand, and I rushed to the street after hearing the explosion."

"Explosion," Feckles said, redoubling his staring. "Was there a bomb, too?"

"No, I meant the gunshot. So, I was on the scene not five minutes after the catastrophe, and had every detail repeated to me."

By now, they had stepped onto the edge of the bridgeway.

"Come, come," Hubner said, stepping farther over the water. "See that approaching carriage? The doomed vehicle stopped just about there. Wait, that's Roost driving. I know him."

Hubner ran up to the carriage and flagged down the vehicle, which was empty of passengers. He fell into a chat with the coachman, pacing along until both halted. "Yes, just here, my good man," Hubner said to Roost, while motioning for the two on the ground to approach. Then, addressing them, he said, "He'll stop here a bit to help out. You two gentlemen climb aboard. Arbuthnot, you to the windward, representing the lady."

With some reluctance, with some hesitation, they climbed aboard, bestowing themselves somewhat uncomfortably in the shabby carriage. Hubner talked over their misgivings. "As it happened, there had been a traffic holdup at the turnoff. The ducal carriage was delayed. Then Kugelmann—I'll take the part of Kugelmann," Hubner ended, moving toward the carriage, pushing aside a few gawkers. "Here, Roost, hand me your whip for just a moment. We can take this for his rifle."

Arbuthnot waved his hand. "But I heard the baron was shot with a pistol."

"Yes, of course, what am I saying?" Hubner came back, correcting himself and wagging the whip. "This is my *pistola*."

Strollers had to take care to weave around the gesticulating policeman, while carriages stalled behind them were starting to protest.

Hubner shouted, "We'll be moving along in a moment. Police business. Allow me one more minute here, if you please."

The glassy water beside and below them was throwing sparkles against the carriage's low ceiling.

"Feckles, be so good as to set well back in your seat, and now Arbuthnot, lean forward as if you saw a friend out the other side of the coach. That was just the opening Kugelmann was awaiting as he paced a few steps behind the carriage. He sprang forward like a Siberian tiger to claw his unfaithful mate. Quickly, there, and I—" With the last pronoun, Hubner bounced forward and jumped on the carriage step, surprising the horses, which made a jostling forward step.

"We caught it. We caught it," Hubner said, stepping back down and motioning for the others to exit the carriage. "You see the reciprocal movements. She moved forward as if to wave to an acquaintance; her husband pulled back."

Hubner had helped the two gentlemen down and now stood, arms akimbo, still blocking the line of pedestrians, while Roost got his buggy underway. Then he about-faced and led them back off the bridge.

Feckles asked, "So, earlier you said there was counterevidence." The trio stepped aside to let a frilly carriage turn in front of them.

"Today, I found out there is a new element in the case. While in jail, this lovesick pacifist was housed with a pair of hardboiled, Bakuninist fanatics. Could it be his time in prison shifted his view, making him, like them, an advocate of what they call 'cleansing violence'?"

The three paused at the next bridge to let a carriage pass.

Hubner kept on, "So when Kugelmann was transferred to Karlsbad and learned that Van Winkle was here, it may be, now influenced by the anarchists, he was determined on revenge."

"What did he have against the American?" Arbuthnot asked, continuing to pepper the officer with questions. He noticed that Feckles seemed distracted, leaving the conversation mentally while he continued to walk at their side.

"Van Winkle makes a particularly vicious bayonet. It's the one that was used in a bayonet charge, three years ago, on a peaceful anti-Hungarian protest in Zagreb. Van Winkle even bragged about the killing efficiency of his product, which proved its mettle at its first test in this massacre. I heard Kugelmann's brother died on that black-letter day. I conjecture he broke out of jail just to get revenge on this supplier of the Hungarian guards."

"I can think of plenty of other reasons a convict would want to escape a noose," Arbuthnot cut back.

"Perhaps so," Hubner said obligingly. "But not these Serbian fanatics. They are in a hurry to die as martyrs, since they imagine the granite statues that will be erected to commemorate their brutality."

"But," Arbuthnot kept on, picking at his argument, "once he heard Van Winkle was visiting, he crashed out as easily as if God were helping him. Weren't there some extraordinary coincidences, a fruit cart turning over on top of his military guard?"

"Very perceptive, doctor. There is no evidence as yet that his escape was anything but an accident, yet I have no doubt that his breakout was assisted by one branch of the Serbian patriots. It was either the reformers to whom he once belonged or the violent wing to which some say he has now pledged allegiance. We don't know what color stripes he had."

"Good metaphor," Arbuthnot commented.

Hubner said modestly, "I'm a poet at heart."

Arbuthnot and Feckles began walking uphill away from the riverfront road. Hubner was about to part from them when he seemed to remember another line of questioning. "You must have known Van Winkle fairly well, doctor," he said, addressing Feckles.

"I've seen him only a few times this summer. Why do you say that?" Feckles answered.

"I heard he complained about your methods. Perhaps, he was offended by your nature cultists' ideas: nude bathing, barbells, nude hiking, even bathing in the waters of the pump room."

Feckles laughed. "Don't give Arbuthnot the wrong impression. We don't walk naked in the wilderness. We wear loincloths. And our jaunts are not coed."

With that, Hubner went on his sprightly way, and the other two walked a little on a branching, upwardly inclined street. The route was mildly overcrowded with parasoled strollers and overstocked with tourist traps, a small series of shops and cafés that ended where a pocket park opened up a little ahead.

Among the cafés was the Parisian, which had somehow been allowed, French style, to put a few tables on the sidewalk. And there sat Smallweed, greeting them as they passed.

Arbuthnot, slowing as he walked and leaning more heavily on his stick, brought up something said in passing in the conversation with the policeman. "Now the Freudenbergs, *père et fils*, you were discussing: were their liver complaints similar to mine?" The unlit cigar still wagging out of his mouth, Arbuthnot leaned forward to hear the answer.

"Freudenberg *fils*'s problem is in his liver. Your complaint is centered in the skin," the doctor replied peremptorily.

"That hardly seems possible. My inflammations ..." Arbuthnot lowered his voice an octave, as if going into medical complaints on the street were a trifle indelicate. He didn't appreciate that Karlsbad in high season was analogous to a battlefield, open-air operating theater in which young doctors hung over the railings, watching, say, a young soldier having his leg amputated, commenting as freely on the surgeon's knife work as they might on the merits of boxers in a prize ring.

Arbuthnot continued, sotto voce, "My boils, carbuncles, and knotty skin arise from internal disturbances. My London physician has described the process."

"Ah, jolly England. I tell you, the British physicians are all salt-and-butter men."

"Meaning?"

"They see the symptoms and even their organic causes, but nothing is buttressed by philosophy. They know not *Naturphilosophie*."

"You mentioned that."

They had reached the small park, which Arbuthnot observed was as wretchedly bare of sheltering trees as his other favorite haunt. All the trees were huddled far away across a plain of grass. "Let's rest a bit on this bench, shall we?" Feckles said, sitting down, perhaps noting Arbuthnot seemed a bit winded. A stone cavalryman, without mount, offered a segment of shade.

"The English doctors know not the deep surface."

"And what may that be?" Arbuthnot said, lowering himself to the hard bench, with a brilliant sky stoking behind them.

"Our skin can be viewed, analogically, as a tariff gate, regulating imports and exports."

Arbuthnot said tentatively, "The internal exhalations, the exports, from my warped liver are causing extrusions."

"You know," Feckles said, shifting in his seat and turning the conversation, "we are quite close to the pump room here. They have a small examination room. I would like to take your pulse and do a brief look-over."

Arbuthnot was agreeable, so they set off, turning around and retreating a quarter-block before ascending some trifling stairs to start off on a thin corridor of a street.

Soon enough, they had come to the pump room, into which patients were streaming as if the bloody work of the morning was long ago. Viewed through the frosted panes of the walls, dimpled by the setting sun, the human outlines inside had a scarlet cast, so that one might think, as was said about the Teplá, that a killing reddened the surroundings.

They squeezed past the line, and Feckles went up to an attendant, the same Frau Dussell who had been on scene for the morning's violence, and asked if they could use the small examination room, the one off the back courtyard.

Dussell said smilingly, "Begging your pardon, but the room is occupied at the moment, but it should be ready shortly. If you could just rest on a bench for a bit." This was accompanied by an apologetic curtsy.

"Well," Feckles said, spying one of his patients, an aged dowager, queuing up for her glass. "Dr. Arbuthnot, you just wait a moment while I have a word with Lady Maple."

He hurried over to her. Arbuthnot surveyed the scene. Most of the benches were filled by quaffers who'd had their dose and were now chatting. He noted one bench, near the front, was illuminated by an odd oblong of sunlight, and looking up, he saw the ceiling had a few panes missing. Perhaps that was connected to the day's crime. Walking down a little, he came upon a bench barely big enough to fit one person. The minute he took his seat, Dussell plopped down beside him.

"Do you mind?" she apologized. "With all the commotion and cleaning up today, I am working a double shift. I just have to get off these dogs a minute."

"Be at your ease," Arbuthnot said.

"You had quite a day, sir."

"Come again?"

"I heard Kugelmann fell right into your arms."

"Why do you say that?"

"The maids say the man was exhausted after he climbed that wall. He could no longer hold himself up and you had to support him."

"You've been misinformed, *mein Liebling*. It's not that my arms served no purpose. I ended up catching both Frau Feckles and her lady's maid when they fainted at the sight of Kugelmann crashing through the windowpanes." He bent reality a little by adding that last flourish about the panes.

"I know it's not right to question guests, but as you know, I was a party to the scene myself. That's why, I suppose, people have told me so many crazy things."

He glanced over at her. She did seem overheated, her hair washed a little with gray. She was older than she at first appeared. The bright white of her uniform smock was soiled.

"What things?"

"Well," she said, then glanced around at the patients, all with their backs or bustles turned toward her, most gabbing loudly and excitedly, some with fixed stares at one point on the ground near the front basin. Presumably, this was where Molly's body was found.

Dussell lowered her voice another few steps. "Let us to go in English. Mine is not so perfect, but safer way."

Arbuthnot nodded assent.

She said, "I heard Kugelmann, he's dying and said something so mysterious." When Arbuthnot didn't respond as he sat thinking over the scene, she pushed again. "Did you happen remark what he said?"

"My God, I was the only one there. Item: the only one awake, and I testify he said nothing."

"And did he point anything?"

"Why would he do that?"

She glanced around warily to make sure, it seemed, no one was eavesdropping. "Just that I heard these rumors he escaped because he must destroy evidence."

"I know nothing about this."

"Idle talk, I guessed."

But then Arbuthnot remembered something, causing her nearly to sink to the floor when he mentioned it. "Come to think of it, he did seem to be pointing as he fell. At the time, I thought he was saluting."

She gasped, "At what?"

"Can't say. Something in the bookcase."

Dussell was increasingly furtive. "We are known the police almost broke him. You see, in Vienna they respect him as noble one, but once they transfer here for execution, some of the jailers give him screwed thumb."

To Arbuthnot, this seemed out of a penny dreadful like the one he had once caught Eleanor reading.

She kept going. "They almost talked him. That's why must have escape. In some book place was list."

"And he went looking for it in the Feckleses' house? That hardly seems reasonable."

"Feckles was his doctor before he killed wife. A trustworthy thing."

It was as if Arbuthnot had opened a garden gate expecting to see well-trimmed flowerbeds and instead found a mass of brambles. "Are you a sympathizer yourself?"

"Mother Serb, but I don't believe in all this bombs, not like some."

"Some?"

She stood up. "My break time is over." She was back to German.

"Are there other Serbians working here?" Arbuthnot asked, looking for illumination.

"Most of us will have nothing to do with these evil extremists. Even Swandra—you know her, she waits on your daughter—even she disapproves."

"Why mention her in particular?"

Looking vexed with herself and holding her mouth so tightly it appeared she were going to bite her tongue off, but, excited as she was pregnant with a juicy tidbit, Dussell came out with it: "Don't noise it around, but Swandra is Kugelmann's half sister."

The news gave her the chance to flounce a little, throwing a ripple into her soiled skirt as she returned to her duties. Meanwhile Feckles passed right in front of Arbuthnot's seat to accost another physician, saying, "Are you finished with the examination room *finally*?"

Arbuthnot thought, *No love lost between these two.*

"Yes," the other doctor returned, just as frostily. "My patient is just dressing."

Feckles conducted Arbuthnot to the back courtyard, where they stood among the broken crates and drying uniforms, waiting for the small examination room to empty. Its door banged open and produced ... Dr. Cranky.

Chapter 8

Earlier that day, Sherlock, after scampering down from his embarrassing perch on the roof of the pump room, had an equally embarrassing talk with his parents, who disdained his apologies as they stood in the dirty back space of the building, confronting a foreman. The man said he hated to upset guests but damaged glass cost money, which they would have to cover. Following that, his father laid down the law, saying that for the remainder of their stay at the sanitarium, Sherlock would be chaperoned by the maid who had traveled with them, the censorious Fidge. Everything appeared drastically bleak till Hubner appeared and cleared things up. First addressing the foreman, Hubner apologized for asking Sherlock to mount up to the roof, implying he didn't expect him to clamber out on the glass, but that was within his rights as a temporarily deputized investigator. With this, he talked the employee down, insisting the owners would have to eat the costs as this was an unavoidable accident of a murder investigation.

Hubner went on, addressing the parents, to say Sherlock's straying out on the glass, even his breaking through the panes, aided him, showing what would have happened to Kugelmann if he had attempted to pass across the roof. This was solid evidence.

"Hard facts," Sherlock threw in.

Hubner concluded by extolling reenactments as a vital part of police work.

This deflated his father's anger a trifle, seeing no money was lost. Once Hubner adroitly turned his attention to

Sherlock's parents, Holmes senior went from high dudgeon to a satisfied complacency, for, after all, wasn't his son helping the authorities?

No, no, father explained to son after Hubner left, Fidge could be left out of it. Oblivious as his father had first seemed to anything but the damage, the impropriety, and the recklessness of his son, now, with Hubner's timely intervention, he had come over to a new, elevated understanding of Sherlock's actions.

The family situation was patched up further when Sherlock pointed out he had only jumped to Hubner's commands because he'd realized the man was a special friend of Mycroft. (Mycroft was the darling boy of the family.)

In any case, what did it matter, what did any crow eaten and insult swallowed matter while, all that time, under fire, the ticket to the Hunter's Ball hung in his pocket? That clue, divulged to no one, would be Sherlock's torch, held high as he made his way through the labyrinth where the secret to this crime lay.

When Sergeant Cuff was a young rookie, his work had constantly been found wanting by that "gruffian" Lieutenant Baldus, just as, in a less gentlemanly way perhaps, Sherlock had often received rough handling from Dr. Arbuthnot over his mistakes in reasoning. He couldn't help thinking Arbuthnot and his crony Cranky were stifling laughs when they listened to him. Then, when young Cuff found a vital clue in "The Mystery of the Green Baize Door," he finally gained Baldus's full approbation.

So, all this time as Sherlock nodded, apologized, and appeared most penitent, his mind kept darting out a set of previews of what the rest of the day should be.

Once he was exonerated and well clear of the family counsel, he made his way to a park bench, where he could map out a plan of action. His thoughts were interrupted by Hubner, who unexpectedly appeared and invited him to take a glass at the Strudel Haus.

The café was an intimate room with only a score of tables. The walls were arranged to look like a collection of door frames within which, on the top and bottom halves where the wood panels would go, were lithographs depicting the Lovers' Catapult Bridge and other mountain views. Near the door to the kitchen, a case of pastries and uncut cakes were heaped with fruits and sugar. Beside that and, as Sherlock had noticed on a previous visit with his parents, more frequently attended to by the patrons, was a large rack of newspapers and journals of opinions. Each customer would go there to select his reading material even before ordering.

When the two entered, they found only one other table occupied. There sat that suspicious fellow Pricklestone. As soon as they came in, he called for his bill.

They ordered coffees, Sherlock asking for some floating cream on top. Hubner took the boy further into his confidence. "I told you before, Mary Van Winkle had been caught literally red-handed."

"Open and shut," Sherlock said as he adjusted the out-of-alignment sugar bowl and napkins, placing everything in good order as the waitress brought the tray with two piping hot cups and two glasses of water.

"Lean closer," Hubner instructed. "Even with the evidence against her, I'm bothered by the suspicious characters I keep running across." With a near-invisible swivel of his thumb, Hubner indicated Pricklestone, who was still paying his bill.

"That character?" Sherlock asked in a low voice.

"Yes, and he's not the worst of them. Also in town is the greatest renegade in the British empire."

Sherlock fell back in his chair. "You don't say. But who would that be?"

"Karl Marx, the man behind the Paris Commune. He's the man I would like you to spy on."

Sherlock was incredulous. "That's a tall stick. How would I find him?"

"Just look around your table at dinner tonight."

"You mean?"

"Dr. Arbuthnot is none other than the red revolutionary, who may very well have had a hand in the killings."

"I say," was Sherlock's first reaction. He went on, "But where does he enter in?"

"What if, for the moment, we assume Mary Van Winkle is not a knife-wielding villainess, but is telling the truth?"

"What's her story?" Sherlock asked.

"On the fatal morning, she had a fight with her husband and stormed out of the pump room. Then she heard the maid scream. She rushes back and finds Molly in a pool of blood. She has to turn her over, as the maid has fallen on the blade. Not thinking, Mary pulls out the weapon, trying to revive the maid, who is still alive."

"What is the husband doing all this time?" Sherlock wondered.

"He was standing there shaking as if he had the palsy. No help at all. Totally overcome. With no help from that quarter, Mary ran to find the police."

Sherlock filled in the dots. "Leaving the husband unharmed?"

"Precisely," Hubner said, taking a tiny sip from his cup before ladling in the sugar. "Now we go to Cranky's account. He looked through the frosted glass of the pavilion and saw the killer, a man in a wolf mask."

"And you think Marx? Do you have any hard facts?"

"A handful." Each time Hubner listed one, he tapped his spoon against his coffee cup. "Marx was seen that morning walking arm in arm with Cranky as they made their way to the pump room. Marx—this is Mary's testimony—walked past their group, looking death daggers at her husband. Lastly, in print Marx has cried out for Van Winkle's head." With the last proof, he clanged his spoon even louder.

"But how did he swing that?"

Hubner didn't seem to have worked out that part, so Sherlock answered, thinking aloud, "You know, although I didn't recognize him, my brother has filled me in on the background of this Marx. Don't forget that the London police, who have taken his measure, don't bother him. He lives free and easy in London.

"It's true that when he was young, he was a crazed pistol, calling for the destruction of the rich and churning out manifestos; yet all his great visions and call for unbridled attacks on the reigning powers fell to the ground.

"For the last few years, as brother Mycroft tells me, he has been shoveling through books in the British Library, building an elaborate verbal labyrinth with the minotaur surplus value sitting in the middle. Any worker foolish enough to enter this *Capital* will wander its unlighted passages for years."

"You are forgetting," Hubner interrupted, "Marx's directing of the International, an organization of hardened miscreants, who are wire-pulling behind every outbreak of riot and rapine across the globe, reaching even as far as China."

"Rank mythology," Sherlock said, snorting in the way his brother did. "The real hot cog in that organization was the anarchist Bakunin, who got himself expelled. Without him, the organization fell to pieces. Now it's just a talking shop with its only functioning group in America, filled with Irish day laborers and Black butlers and maids."

The youth ended, "The name International is now but a name to frighten burghers and baby dolls."

Hubner took a long draw on his coffee. "Even if the fellow is as much the clawless kitten you claim, he still bears watching. That's why I asked you here. Do you think you could keep an eye on him and report to me?"

"Rather."

~

After the two had parted, Sherlock, moving with a new sense of purpose—wait till Mycroft heard his brother had been trailing Marx—went back to his early thoughts about following out the clue of the ball ticket he'd found on the roof. He kept its existence to himself, as he had already devised a means of finding its significance.

Sherlock reasoned that even if it turned out Mary or Marx had committed the crimes, the mystery of the ball ticket had not been solved. Someone had been using the roof as a listening post, and it could hardly have been Kugelmann, who would not have had a ticket to the Hunter's Ball. The spying must have been done recently, as the chits had only been issued in the last few days.

So what was the voyeur's object? The roof was directly opposite the Feckleses' apartment, the toyshop, and the storage building. Sherlock guessed the convict was hiding in one of these places, leading to the odd conjecture: Could it be the peeper was looking at Kugelmann?

Sherlock's first visit in pursuit of this clue would be to the prison, where he would interview Kugelmann. The youth was smiling, keen as mustard as he went along the cobblestoned streets and alleys to the jail.

Though small in stature, the prison was imposing enough, standing out from the bright pastels of the burghers' houses and shops and from the less plumaged but much statued and decorated white buildings that enclosed the spa facilities. This place was gray and faceless as a wall, having no lower windows and a single anonymous door, fronted by a sentry.

He approached the man. "Do you know me?"

That received a blank stare.

"I think you know my brother," Sherlock said, and he thought, why not add a spurious title, which Bohemians loved so much. "My brother, Police Chief Mycroft Holmes, visited here last year as part of the English delegation."

"I met him," the stolid-faced trooper replied.

"So, since I was visiting with my parents, my brother asked me, if it was not too much trouble, to talk to his friend the jailer a little about conditions in your prison, which I hear are excellent."

With a seeming reluctance, the sentry admitted him.

Going in, the boy felt almost squeezed, having left the spacious square in front of the building to enter a receiving area that seemed little bigger than a cloakroom. It was narrow, appropriately enough for a house of confinement. Directly in front was a desk; on facing sides, doors. The man seated by the desk was a small, birdlike figure, bent over a writing tablet, scratching away like a parakeet sorting through seed at the bottom of its cage. He was so absorbed, or pretended to be, that he didn't look up till he finished copying a long sentence.

His first words: "I recognize you."

That was a lucky stroke.

"Yes, Sergeant Hubner introduced us," Sherlock began. "In fact, I come here as an errand boy. The good sergeant is deep in the case. He requested I ask Kugelmann a few questions." Then, as if casually and assured of the functionary's assent: "Is the prisoner in his quarters now?"

"No."

Sherlock didn't expect such a reply. "But why not?"

The man looked up with an unreadable grimace. "We don't keep corpses in cells."

"What are you saying?"

"Kugelmann was poisoned. He was nearly dead when we brought him in. That's why he collapsed when he toppled in Mrs. Feckles's grate." The policeman glanced about. "I shouldn't say so much, but I was introduced to you by a dear colleague, who assured me you are a good chap."

If he would say so much, perhaps he would say more, Sherlock thought. Though his first line of investigation was stymied, he quickly leapt to another point of attack. "I guess we will never know," Sherlock said carefully, "about Kugelmann's involvement in the Van Winkle murder, just as we will never know who helped him break free from detention. That's—"

He wasn't allowed to finish. "It was all a damnable coincidence, not planned, not organized. Damned annoying the way this dog kept wiggling out of his collar."

While this might have seemed the preface to further remarks, the man followed up by bending back over his report, dipping his pen in an inkhorn that resembled nothing so much as a bird feeder.

Sherlock tried to distract him from becoming immersed in his duties by supplying information he would rather have heard, with embellishments, from the clerk. "I know this political murder took place a couple of years ago and, due to the gravity of the case, was tried in Vienna. It was thought that since the crime was here, then the execution had to be here as well. Only fitting."

Sherlock realized he had been, almost comically, slowing down his talk as if he were a windup doll running down, expecting the functionary to jump in any moment.

"Two weeks ago"—it was actually ten days—"Kugelmann was to be driven"—they actually walked—"to the court hard by"—it was actually at the far end of town—"at high noon"—it was actually dawn.

What is wrong with this knucklehead? Sherlock thought when the man looked up.

"I let you continue because you are retailing what you read in our press. These journalists are notorious bunglers."

He let Sherlock dangle for a minute, the boy thinking, *Well, is he going to set them right?*

He did. "It was closer to ten days ago than two weeks that this transpired, and Kugelmann was walked to the court, which is all the way over by the Bristol Sanitarium. And he left at dawn, not noon, so as to avoid traffic and interference. Yes, that's when the string of unlucky breaks began.

"An ignorant market woman. Everyone knows her. She's the bath attendant Frau Dussell's grandmother. She was unloading fruit from a horse-driven cart. Something spooked the horse; he shifted and the pull trailer fell over, spilling a ton of fruit, knocking down the guards, one even being brained by a cauliflower. Kugelmann, backing away, and he's a strong one, clubbed down two unmowed-over guards with his arm chains and was off."

"There was a chase?"

"There would have been if half the men weren't pinned under the cart and many others unconscious or with legs nearly broken by fallen cantaloupes."

"I guess the grandmother was bewildered."

"Bewildered and jailed."

"But I thought she wasn't considered culpable."

"Bringing a very road-unworthy cart into Karlsbad is a gross violation. And breaking ribs and crushing skulls with watermelons is punishable negligence."

Sherlock poised, not daring to say anything or even move lest he stop the man's narration.

"The fellow was itching to escape and finish his mission."

Daring one word, Sherlock whispered, "Mission?"

"Somehow, he found out the millionaire Henry Van Winkle was in town. This damned plutocrat supplied weapons to the Austrian soldiers who slew Kugelmann's friends in the Serb revolutionary circle. He wanted revenge. That's what gave him the strength to grab that chance and battle his way past the guards."

Shifting back from affability to parakeet-like attention, the clerk lowered his head and became absorbed again in his scratching. Saying an unheard goodbye, Sherlock was back on the pavement, where he exchanged a pleasant remark with the sentry and redirected himself to the pump room.

~

With Kugelmann sealed in the grave, short of a séance, the kind his mother attended, there was now no way to ascertain if he had known anything about the spy on the pump room roof. Sherlock still wondered if the convict had actually been hidden across the street. As Sherlock had hinted when talking at table, Kugelmann had been seen between the second and third stories of the building. No one had picked up his hint, instead, as Marx and Cranky did so often, dismissing anything he said. His hint was that maybe Kugelmann's climb didn't originate on the street but from a second-story perch.

So, the best investigatory course would be to get to the two second-floor rooms and test for signs of occupancy.

Sherlock had to admit it had been a deuced dodgy day. In the course of a few hours, he had learned that the crime he was investigating had already been sewed up by the police; that he was dining nightly with a legendary criminal mastermind, now in retirement; and that a third murder had already come to light.

It couldn't be that Kugelmann had committed suicide. Why kill yourself when you can just turn yourself in and become a martyr for Serbian independence? It must be that someone had poisoned him. Actually, he realized for casuists this offered an admirable puzzle. Say a criminal were being driven through the streets on an open cart, a tumbril, as they used to do in London, on his way to be hanged. A man emerged from the crowd and shot him dead. Would that new man be tried for murder?

But why was he killed? Had Kugelmann seen something from where he was concealed? And where could he have been concealed? If he was ascending to the third floor, which second floor had sheltered him?

This confounded Marx had a way of discussing things that was clinically clean, mathematical, something he must have learned swotting in the British Library. In examining the possibilities of a situation, you take a combinatory box and plug in every solution by tumbling around the elements. It might work here.

Sherlock had noticed that the two second-floor windows that could have served the cat climber were those of a toyshop and that of the pump room's storage area. So, to work the combinatory, Kugelmann either broke into or was let into the storage room *or* he either broke into or was helped into the toyshop. Sherlock had just learned that Heidi might have been connected to Kugelmann's escape, and she probably had prepared a place to hide in the storage building. The toyshop seemed a less likely haven, although Sherlock knew little enough about the place and its owner, François.

Sherlock always kept about his person a few innocuous-looking detective aids, one of which, a jeweler's loupe, he palmed as he came near to the bustling entrance of the pump room. His object was the pump room's storage site, diagonally in front of the spa facility's entrance. It was the chatter of the throng lined up at that entrance that he trusted would cover his investigation.

What he wanted to start with was a hasty but thorough examination of the lock of this room and of the adjoining store. The youth's reasoning here was that if Kugelmann had forced the door to one of these chambers, some evidence would be left of his jimmying.

Bending over as if to inspect the lovely doorknob of the pump room's storage area and with a concealing hand fixing the loupe to his eye, Sherlock quickly ascertained there had been no evident attacks on this lock. He righted himself and walked casually over to the toyshop. He summoned up another key trait of the master detective: patience. He pretended to be studying the toy soldiers on display since at the millinery shop, just beyond, a fräulein with a strawberry complexion, a freshet of pretty dimples, and straw-colored hair was gazing lovingly at a feathered hat, standing one step from the toyshop entrance.

The tin men Sherlock glanced at were not in random rows, but, as he saw, arranged to memorialize a famous battle, a triumph that set a glow in his English heart. In the window, the British were holding back Napoleon's troops. Pushed back into a narrowing defile, his country's infantry held position. He studied their crisp uniforms: red coats with the slash of the white powder belt diagonally across their breasts. Heads in brimless stovepipes. They were firing "at will," some shooting, some loading, some taking aim. The French grenadiers, pouring down from a slight rise, were wearing their short blue coats with double straps crossing their fronts, red epaulets, and large, plumed head-pieces. They were firing as they ran, some war-whooping, and behind them, riding into the scene, were the chasseurs, with their brilliant bright-red capes fluttering out.

What a sight. Sherlock picked out the British commander, a little back from the ragged line. He imagined the man urging the men to stand like bricks, for if the line broke, they were doomed. "Keep your eyes to your work," he growled. "Uh." The soldier directly in front of the lieuten-ant had been hit in the breast. He stumbled back into the officer's arms, his head swiveling up so he registered his leader's face. His expiring words: "For king and country, sir."

Just then, from behind them, *Kaboom!* A rattling good blast lit in the middle of the advancing French. "Our twelve-pounders," the green officer yelled. As the cannonballs kept coming, the French turned tail, and a cheer went up from the redcoats. "Hurrah for Georgie!"

The fräulein, the woman too near the toyshop door, was summoned by a friend and trotted off. But that didn't leave the space clear. The new intruder was someone he knew by sight: Yvette, an all-work maid attached to the hotel. Out of uniform, at first, she seemed to be window gazing, but it turned out she had an actual destination, François's Toyshop. The proprietor, noticing her approach, came to the door and, strange behavior for a shop proprietor, barred her entrance.

François was quite elegantly dressed for a toy purveyor. He sported a deep blue jacket and matching vest and dark pants. He looked self-satisfied, even smug, behind his close-trimmed black beard.

"My pet," he said in French, glancing at Holmes, who acted as if he were enthralled by the miniatures, pretending not to understand the foreign language. "My pet, you can't go upstairs. This is not the time."

"But I want to gaze at it once more."

"I told you, sweetness, tonight a few of our sympathy will gather to look upon it."

"One peek."

He pushed her back. "Come again at eleven, and don't be late."

As each increasingly mysterious statement came in their talk, Sherlock scowled more and leaned closer to the glass, feigning he was absorbedly trying to pick out some detail on the battlefield.

And he was absorbed, not by the diorama but by the secrets and conspiracies he overheard as the two discussed the upstairs room. And in a way, they were also addressing their remarks to him. After all, hadn't they made an appointment for this evening? One he vowed to keep.

Chapter 9

While the dinner was quite festive now that Cranky had rejoined the party and as it was a prelude to going to hear an outdoor concert, Sherlock had trouble getting into the jolly mood, since he had learned Eleanor and her father were here under false pretenses.

He listened noncommittally as Cranky told the story of his release. "This Sergeant Hubner is a quick man. They have put him in charge of the investigation. He walked in, threw me a tennis ball, and released me."

"On what grounds?" Sherlock asked.

"Aside from Heidi's testimony that I was with her when the crime was perpetrated, he could tell from the wounds that the crime was done by a right-handed killer. I caught the toss with my left hand."

"He sounds like a sound reasoner," Sherlock said.

"Little did he know, I'm ambidextrous," Cranky came back.

That rated a good laugh at the policeman's expense, which all joined. Sherlock imagined only his own chuckle was put on.

The main course was served, and it was only after it was tucked away that Sherlock returned to the topic. "Cranky, you said you had seen some disguised man in the pavilion, so I wonder if anyone was lurking around. Dr. Arbuthnot, did you see anyone?"

"Why name me?" Marx replied, pushing his chair back so he could sit more comfortably.

Sherlock disguised the source of his information. "I was up early this morning and saw you leaving the hotel with Dr. Cranky."

Marx, leaning back farther, said, "Come to think of it, I did see that mysterious fellow Pricklestone pass me as I neared the embankment. Why was he up so early? I heard he's not here for the cure."

Cranky threw in, "Maybe his ailment is an anemic fortune. He always seems to be at the gaming table."

The conversation passed on to other topics, and after dessert, which for Sherlock was peaches with a dab of the special floating cream the Bohemians made so well, they walked to the space where the concert would be performed.

En route, Cranky told his friends that as he left the prison, he met Dr. Feckles, himself on his way out. The physician had been called in to make some preliminary deductions on what poison had finished the villain. As Feckles reported, Hubner was especially interested in how long the poison would have taken to act.

Cranky went on, "Dr. Feckles believes Kugelmann was killed with colchium. I don't know much about poisons, but—"

Sherlock stepped in verbally. "It's a plant derivative from crocuses, used to make a salve, I believe, that is a treatment for gout."

They had reached the concert space, and Cranky waved his hand as the group settled into lawn chairs. They were sitting down about four rows back from the front. Sherlock took over, saying, "Let me say a few things about colchium, as the pharmacology of poisons is something of a hobby of mine.

"Colchium takes effect in one or two hours after administration. If you mixed it in water, it would dissolve and might be drunk by the unsuspecting. If it were in the atmosphere, you could breathe it in. As it works through the body, it ends by causing a terrible thirst in the victim and then stops the breath."

Eleanor put in, "Could it be Kugelmann was acting for the Serbs and—wasn't he a martyr type—he took the poison himself so he couldn't be made to testify against those who hid him and helped him escape?"

"Tut, tut," Marx said. "Don't be a dummkopf, Tussy. You are forgetting the killer wore an animal mask. Why would a known killer have to conceal his face?"

Sherlock thought of something. "But didn't Kugelmann have a very theatrical streak? Perhaps he put on the mask just to make his presence more frightening."

～

The music began.

It was being performed in a large space filled with rows of chairs in the area between two hotels. Rather than facing toward the back of the square, their seats were turned toward the dining room of the Hotel Thermal, whose windows had been opened so a small orchestra could be placed inside. Perched around them were middle-class matrons with their husbands and broods, dressed to show their wealth or taste or, in some cases, neither. A few music-loving dowagers and noblemen had also slipped in, including the fantastic wife of Minister Haupt, who had been attacked by a flea this morning.

It began, under able baton of bandmaster Strauss. The first piece would be the premiere of a new arrangement of Mozart's "Divertimento 10 in F major," done by and extended by a Viennese modernist, who had added horns to the original violins, cello, and viola. Strauss told them, "This entrancing music will move your hearts and change your minds."

It started with an allegro. One violin moved lightly over the short, sharp intrusions of the horns and other strings as if it were a leaf, so gossamer, it slid, pitching, over a pond's surface. It lit a tracery, sometimes above, sometimes under the low scrim of notes, at moments being swept up and joining the general chorus. The allegro kicked off brusquely, in full motion, as if one had entered a sporting ground planning to view the first race only to see the horses crossing the finish line.

Then the andante. After a light, stately promenade, ornamented by an influx of tiny trills, which made it slightly giddy, the two horns entered distantly, fox hunters far over the hills. Then the tempo advanced, two lines reverberating in counterpoint, two sustained high notes, followed by a series of tones moving up the scale toward the memory of those sustained notes, moving fluently, graciously, as if pulled up by cords.

Sherlock, who was no mean violinist himself, thought of leaves racing across a pond, and somehow their easy flight, the fluidness of the musical passage, suggested that he should himself let his ideas float out, not demarcating, in a selfish way, what he thought from what others thought. Moreover, he had such differently capable companions, each of whom, like a musical instrument, offered something distinctly personal. Therefore, if they would, following his example, generously share their thoughts, it was near inevitable (as he saw it) that they would achieve victory over the forces of darkness. He must reveal the existence of the ball ticket to his friends.

Meantime, Eleanor listened intently as strings slid down the scale, then, undergoing a fast retrenchment, zigzagged back up to the initial prominence. From there, a promenade took over. The horns would come in, hang around for a few bars, and there would be a pause, one representing the deference of the horns to the strings, standing aside as they took their turn. Suddenly, the two violins played a motive, and then the two other strings joined in with the figures alongside the first instruments as if they were being instructed in a step.

The next movement, as she heard it, opened with two long notes, separated like fence posts by an octave. These were horn contributions. Then a single violin began to play in the range between these two notes as if this were the space cleared for them. This went on for quite a few bars, when the violin broke out of its box and, going head over heels from the confining octave, flew through high notes with insistent chords pushing tidally beneath it. The violins reminded her of a horse jumping a fence. At the end, another startling effect, all the music is quelled and the violin is heard alone, yearning, lower than the original setup, as if this instrument were pining to reenter the trellis of the original octave.

As the horse metaphor occurred to Eleanor, it brought back full force the word picture Yvette had painted of the saucy bet Mary had made about riding Von Pelt's steed. She realized it was such an amusing story—for only in the empty spaces of the music had she been able to consider it—that, though she had hesitated to bring it up, for it bordered on the salacious, she saw it could only achieve its true dimensions if it were retold.

Meanwhile, Marx listened with some appreciation as an andante moved through a hurried, galloping entry, then one pause, and then a single violin note twanged. The juxtaposition of these two themes showed Mozart's—or was it his rearranger's—dry wit. The following sequence was rollicking; two related motives played along, one under the other, but with one starting on a lower octave, finishing, then popping up two octaves above the other line as if the motives were playing leapfrog.

Soon a final andante, moving at breakneck speed, like a gig roaring past, but as in a racecourse, the melody floated in a circle, a circle of fifths, running up and down the notes, first one violin, then a second following, walking in its footsteps.

Something in the amiable cooperation of the musical instruments suddenly provoked Marx to reconsider his thought about sharing information about the underground Serbian independence movement with his fellow "criminologists."

As he saw it, the only doubtful character in their group was Sherlock. Not only had he a policeman brother, but his suspicious question about Marx's whereabouts this morning made him wonder about his motives. Even so, he might present the information about the Serbs simply as knowledge gained from reading the gazette, not from frequenting anarchist soirees.

~

When the concert finished, Eleanor was eager to share what she knew of the piquant picnic scene with her father and Cranky, so she was more displeased than pleased when Sherlock coaxed his parents into letting him accompany his friends to the coffeehouse for a "quick sip." She didn't think she could recount the story in his presence, as it was not suitable for his youthful ears. She had seen him blush at dinner whenever there was a ribald sally from Cranky or father.

So, after they plied their way up a short rise on Petra Velikého, they entered the Vienna Café, a lively meeting place for the musical crowd. The place was noisy, jammed, smoky. A stack of tables sat along two walls under crayon portraits and etchings of prominent Viennese conductors and sopranos. The tables in the center were less preferred by the group, as those seated there had to continually shift as patrons and waiters squeezed between the close-packed furniture. Each table started the evening with a white tablecloth, but as the night proceeded, it would be dappled by spills and notations, sometimes a musical phrase drawn to illustrate a point of argument. Many of the patrons were not simply connoisseurs but actual players or composers who would argue loudly over the merits of Wagner's total music (*gesamtkunstwerk*) or about the delicate stylings of the latest Austrian "songbird."

Despite the loud conversations, passionate outbursts, and sudden warblings when someone illustrated a point by singing it, the four favored this "Bohemian" (in the nongeographic sense) café because, if anything controversial came up, they could talk under the loud banter without being overheard.

They joined the crush and, by their request, stood waiting for a wall placement even while an empty table in the room middle seemed to beckon, as would a finger coming from behind a screen, for these weary souls to sit down. They resisted this call and soon enough obtained a wall table, one with a bust of Liszt encumbering the small enough table space and looked down upon by—was it mockingly?—huge mezzotints of Bizet and Verdi.

After they were seated, Eleanor thought of bringing up her story, toning it down a bit, but Sherlock, again relying on Hubner's information, posed an interesting question. "We've been assuming the Serbs helped Kugelmann escape and hid him up, but we don't have a definite answer as to whether it was planned or accidental."

Father answered first, but in a way to withdraw a candidate. "As I mentioned at table, Swandra was Kugelmann's half sister and may have helped him escape jail; however, I don't think she should be connected to the murder plot."

Sherlock jumped in, saying, "We all know she waits on and has been very kind to your precious daughter, but don't let that sway your opinion."

Father went on, "I've looked into the Serbian independence movement. There are reformist and revolutionary wings. I believe Swandra is a reformist, a gradualist."

Cranky jumped in with, "We do have a candidate for the more militant faction."

Eleanor smiled to herself. She knew Cranky had a wide acquaintance among the maids and hotel girls, so she was not surprised he might have heard gossip about the varied political leanings of the staff.

"Who, exactly?" Sherlock asked.

"I blush to say it," Cranky admitted, "but Fräulein Dussell has more than once voiced strong admiration for the Serbian and even the Russian pan-Slav martyrs who died with bombs in their hands."

Yvette was on her mind, so Eleanor brought her in, saying that while the maid would hardly have had a place to hide Kugelmann, "I once overheard her talking to another maid, talking about the detested reign of Louis Napoleon, which led to the destroying of the Commune and other defeats of progressive movements. I think of her as a militant of some sort."

She knew her remark was off the topic of Serbian independence, but she was trying to bridge her way to telling her picnic anecdote, even if she had to water it down, but the talk veered as her father said, "Sherlock's comment about Kugelmann's theatrical love of melodrama is an important observation, especially connected to Cranky's remark that animal masks were readily available in the storage place. That puts him back on the chessboard."

Eleanor was pleased her father was finally paying attention to what Sherlock said, as he often ignored the youth's comments as if they were said by a passerby.

Everyone had an opinion, and the night flew by. One other comment by her father struck her. He noted, "According to Heidi, Kugelmann may have concealed something important, perhaps a list of revolutionary comrades, in Feckles's apartment, presumably not known to the Feckleses. Could it be that Kugelmann, knowing he was dying of the poison, climbed the wall to make a last-ditch effort to retrieve and destroy this document?"

Soon after this revelation, the conversation broke up, or rather was broken up by a sudden dispute over Wagner among the other patrons. The café had become (metaphorically) two warring camps, which (more literally) were roaring at each other as if exchanging cannonballs: one side declaiming the merits of their champion, the other the musical atrocities of the composer, who had quite lately set up a shrine/graveyard for harmony/Philistines at Bayreuth.

The foursome paid up and left the rowdy atmosphere, taking a winding passageway back to the hotel, which was so narrow they could only walk two abreast. Eleanor was paired with Cranky and, making the best of his love of the off-color, told him the saucy story of Von Pelt, Mary, and their maids during their picnic encounter.

Sherlock interrupted, wanting to ask Cranky more about poisons, so she fell in step with her father, who said he had something for her ears only.

Marx stated, "I had heard the Van Winkle's maid's name a few times, always referred to as Molly, but reading the paper today I got her full name, Molly Peters."

"Is that significant?"

"If I can trust my recall, a Molly Peters was a member of the American branch of the International."

Eleanor barely had time to digest the meaning of this fact when Cranky tapped her father on the shoulder to engage him in conversation.

Now she was in front with Sherlock, who surprised her by asking her to walk a little faster so they could put a distance between them and the other two. Once they had moved ahead, Sherlock blurted, "The police know your father's secret identity."

Eleanor shuddered convulsively, a reaction that sometimes preceded a faint. She steeled herself as Sherlock raced to reassure her, saying in one breath, "Don't worry. They have no intention of deporting him or making trouble. They have their hands full."

He took a second breath. "I defended your father to Sergeant Hubner, explaining he was only visiting Karlsbad to take the cure." He paused, then said, "I did it for your sake, Miss Eleanor. I don't want you upset."

"That's not it. That's not it at all," she declaimed.

"What, then?"

"Don't let Daddy know about this. He just has so many things: the illness, the ..." *Why not say it?* she thought to herself, since Sherlock was privy to their secret. "... the breakup of the International, the collapse of the Paris Commune."

"I won't tell your father what I know," the boy said.

Eleanor stopped them and, glancing back to see how far they were ahead, suddenly reached out and took both his hands and, staring strongly into his gray eyes, said, "You have to promise. Promise with all your heart."

Chapter 10

Another utensil every detective must keep at all times is a pocket telescope. That along with a derringer, which Sherlock's father had gotten him for his birthday and which he kept in his inner pocket.

Sherlock brought his telescope into play as he lay prone like one of the snipers in the British army display in the toyshop window, flat on the top of the pump room, gazing clear-eyed at a curtain across the way.

He hoped but could hardly bet on the toyshop's second-floor drapery being drawn back to reveal the room's secret treasures, but, as a rather minimal compensation, and depending on a third must-have item in the detective's toolkit, he could jot down on his notepad who was in attendance at this after-hours, sub-rosa soirée.

Once François had descended to his shop, Sherlock moved his viewer downward and ticked off the guests as they walked in. All of them, excepting two outliers, had something in common. Yvette, another French maid, and three ill-dressed workmen—one of whom he recognized as a gardener and all of whom he gathered were from Alsace-Lorraine—were French. The first outlier, who didn't fit at all, was Miss Chung, the laundry girl. Then he saw a second odd duck approaching and let out to himself, "What, oh? Here's Swandra approaching. What is she doing mixed with all these Frenchies?"

After everyone was accounted for and the shop's gas globes were turned off, François led them upstairs for their mysterious conclave.

Patience was the detective's cardinal virtue. Stolidly, Sherlock sat, eye glued to a blank wall. Stuffiness was in his favor, he reflected. After a few minutes, Yvette, who apparently didn't appreciate the closeness of the room, pulled back the curtain and raised the sash.

Sherlock had trained himself to engage in the instant mind-plate capture of a scene that appeared for a flash of a second, in this instance, for as long as it took to open the curtains, raise the window, and slide those curtains back together.

What happened was a double unveiling. With her pert face turned, all unknowing, toward him, Yvette yanked back the drapes while simultaneously, as he now saw revealed, François was doing the same with a tarpaulin on the floor. Sherlock saw a large cover, which took up most of the center of the room, being pulled away. That tarp was being pulled off just as Yvette opened the curtains. Under the floor covering was a vast diorama of Paris.

Sherlock first recognized the spire of Notre Dame like a single digit pointing up from the Île-de-France. There was the snaky Seine and the colossal hills of Montmartre and Belleville. But it was a city sadly littered with cotton balls, red tissue paper, and debris: a recreation of the battles during the last days of the Commune. The streets were filled with smaller versions of the tin soldiers seen downstairs, the National Guards trying to repel the Versailles troops from behind improvised barricades. The cotton balls were smoke from artillery pieces, the tissue paper sheets of flame around burning buildings, and the debris from edifices shattered or going down.

The crew in François's rooms crowded around the stationary tableau on all sides, leaning forward and gesticulating as the curtain dropped back into place.

Setting down the telescope, which was wearying to the eye, but not unpinning his gaze from the casement, Sherlock let his mind revolve through a plentiful set of ideas that the scene awakened. The first remark he made to himself was that all these viewers, the Chinese and Swandra not excluded, had likely been Parisians who had evacuated shortly before or even participated in the Paris Commune's last stand.

As Eleanor had told him one evening, during the battle, Versailles units immediately executed anyone captured. Once they won the city, when the Parisians were defeated, they were also humiliated. The conquerors arrested scores, taking thousands on a devil's march back to the Versailles prisons. Gratuitously and fiendishly, officers would stop the prisoners' parade to pull out anyone who caught their eyes and gun them down, letting them tumble into a roadside ditch. Once in the city, the broken men and women walked a gauntlet in which the glittering youth and their fair ladies spit at them, beat them, and laughed at their misery.

Those who took their places in the gauntlet, Eleanor had said, were not simply blasted French conservatives, but foreign visitors who had come to Versailles due to the "open city" atmosphere of anything goes: gambling, drinking, and debauchery. In fact, as his friend had learned, the widow Mary, not married at that time, had been there at the baccarat table and maybe among those in the gauntlet.

Considering this past history and given the secrecy and the lateness of the hour, Sherlock concluded these were ex-Communards, ex-fighters, who had gathered to shed a tear for fallen comrades and perhaps plan small-scale future retaliations. Because of the continuing state repression of any involved in the uprising, it behooved them to keep their get-togethers veiled.

Sherlock continued his thinking and his vigilance, only relaxing when the group trooped downstairs and said their goodbyes an hour later.

He rolled over onto his back. Above him, seen through a kind of gauze created by remaining cloud wisps, he looked on a great sprinkling of stars resembling the sugar drizzled on a browned pancake.

Amidst his stargazing, Sherlock's mind was troubled. He had assured Hubner that Marx could not be involved in any way in these murders. Marx was merely taking the waters, bathing, dining, and reading the papers. But given the man was so connected to the Commune, it was out of the question to think that he wasn't consorting with this secret society.

The Communards were not involved in the murder of the maid and millionaire, true, but the indefatigable Hubner might find out about this nest and make trouble for them and Marx, who must be linked up with them. Sherlock instinctively wanted to protect dear Eleanor, who he thought of as the elder sister he never had.

Thoughts of Eleanor led inexorably to another tender spot in his heart, the one occupied by Yvette. For all the mythology of French coquettes, Yvette seemed, if anything, more prim and restrained than her Bohemian counterparts. He found her type of woman—the quietly held-in personality, more like his father than his mother—strangely attractive. She was much preferable to the Eleanor type, who maintained a general sheen of Victorian propriety when it suited her but, when she saw an opening, might indulge in borderline ribaldry.

He considered what to do. It was evident he had to talk to Eleanor and warn her about the Communards who might have a traceable connection to her father. He should check up on Swandra and find her connection to Paris. He had to talk to Yvette and learn what he could about this group who met secretly to gaze at a diorama. Add to that, he might go to see Herr Wong, the Chinese laundryman.

Sherlock had already met him. The youth had a deep fascination with the Orient. And he acknowledged he was influenced by Oily of the Yard, who had learned many

secrets by visiting London's Limehouse district and looking into Chinese curio shops. So, soon after arriving in
Karlsbad, Sherlock had visited Wong's laundry, where the
man had sold him an invaluable pamphlet, *Mind Control
Methods of the Mandarins*. Wong had also helped Sherlock
with the design for a lovely necklace, which the youth had
brought to be made at a silversmith's. Sherlock imagined
Wong could tell him the background of his employee Miss
Chung, perhaps explaining what had caused her to turn up
at this midnight rendezvous.

Yes, as a good detective, he should do all these things;
however, as a stripling youth with little experience with
the fairer, he had trouble considering this without some
agitation. Sherlock could talk companionably at table with
the distaff sex, even with brash representatives such as
Eleanor, but to arrange a tête-à-tête with a stunning, quietly
charming beauty like Yvette was hindered by ... well. Just
thinking about it he felt he was blushing a mile wide or, to
phrase that another way, he had a reddening of the face as
wide and glittering as the Milky Way standing high above
his head.

Chapter 11

The next morning, combing her locks while sitting at her dressing table in the pleasant dappling of early-morning light coming through her two windows, Eleanor was thinking of Lissagaray when Swandra peeped in.

She was happy to see the maid, as she wanted to interrogate her. Eleanor was facing the mirror, the maid behind her, as Eleanor told her, "I found out poor Kugelmann was your half brother."

The way Swandra was situated, the play of light, the angles of the mirror, made it easy for Eleanor to watch the maid's reflection while her own features could not be easily seen.

With the mention of her dead brother, Swandra's face fell, and it continued in its descent as Eleanor went on. "I know you, along with Heidi, might have helped him escape prison, although not with the purpose of further bloodshed. You are a reformer and peacemaker and had no intention of harming the Van Winkle family."

"I had my reasons for hating them," Swandra replied, her face in reflection scowling over Eleanor's shoulder, taking on a harder expression than Eleanor had ever seen before. Swandra's russet hair was not in its usual bun. A few locks had cut loose and crisscrossed her forehead.

Eleanor asked, "When did this come into the picture? I didn't know you knew the Van Winkles."

Swandra pulled Eleanor's hair roughly as she said, "Mary Van Winkle was throwing over her husband to steal my beau."

Eleanor was surprised, her wonder showing on her own face. "Who was your fiancé?" she asked.

"Captain Von Pelt. We met here in the winter. Even with his military background, he is no ignorant Junker, but a man of refinement."

"Quit pulling my hair," Eleanor squeaked. With the last rough stroke, her face in the mirror had jerked back like that of a badly managed marionette.

She gave her own reading of the situation. "I think you are imagining all this. When a man works in a certain capacity, giving riding lessons to wealthy nincompoops, he has to be deferential, even flirtatious."

"I saw it," Swandra protested. "She was being driven into his arms."

"What are you on about?"

"Mary was friendly with this ardent gamester Pricklestone, and that man was trying to throw her together with the captain."

"I don't see that," Eleanor objected. "I think you are looking at everything with a jealous cat's eye."

Swandra moved her face behind Eleanor's head, where she couldn't be glimpsed in the glass, and said, "I saw them together."

"So you helped your brother escape so he would get revenge on Mary?"

"No, that was a whole different thing. From what I heard, people helped him escape so he could find the Shakespeare."

At least the mention of the Bard seemed to have calmed her combing.

"I'm sorry, my lady, I'm mixing hares and hounds. I'm not myself." An amazingly sharp brushstroke proved that.

Swandra's head poked back in the mirror as Eleanor prodded. "You speak of Shakespeare?"

"It's the play *As You Want It*."

"What about it?" Eleanor asked.

"Just as my brother was plotting his revenge on the baron, he was given a copy of a first-folio Shakespeare by a sympathizer to sell it to raise funds for the cause. He knew when he carried out his deed of love, the police would be on his trail, so if he gave us the book right off, the gendarmes might trace it. He hid it on the Feckleses' bookshelf without them finding out."

"How did he accomplish that, for heaven's sake?" Eleanor asked.

Although she wasn't gazing into a magic mirror, because she had gone with Father to visit the Feckleses' homestead on a number of occasions, Eleanor had no trouble visualizing the scene as Swandra described it.

～

When Dr. Feckles opened the door to Erick Kugelmann, the visitor looked around distractedly rather than face his host.

"What brings you here?"

Erick hemmed and hawed as if he were unsure of his own purposes. Then he came out with, "I want to consult your bookshelf. I am desperately in need of distraction now that my darling ran off with that churl."

"My good man," Feckles said sympathetically, "I can see you are at a low ebb."

Erick was dressed in dun colors with a long coat worn like a cape over his shoulders, open so the dirty green lining was visible. He had on brown Alpine pants that only fell to the knee and prominent gray socks. Everything was set off by a black half-scarf flung flamboyantly around his neck.

The two stood for a moment as if stalled in the anteroom of the apartment. It was jammed with such items as a coat stand, one of the ubiquitous elephant-foot umbrella holders, and boxes of uncrated medical books.

They walked down the short passage to the living room.

Feckles's maid popped out from the kitchen but Feckles waved her away.

"So," the doctor said, "you want to make my house into a lending library?"

That remark didn't rouse any cheer in Erick, who said gloomily, "You know my fiancée was intrigued away from me."

"I've heard talk of that," Feckles responded. "Listen, my wife knows more about matters of the heart than I do, but as a doctor I can tell you lovesickness involves a density of sulphur in the blood."

His dissertation was cut short by a loud rattling, followed by a crash in the kitchen.

"What the dogs has she been getting up to?" Feckles had now become the distracted as he rushed out to the kitchen.

This was the opening Erick had been awaiting. He plucked the Shakespeare from his inner sleeve and placed it on the nearest shelf. He had already pasted a blank cover on the spine, the type found on many medical books.

∽

After Swandra finished telling the story, Eleanor asked her how she knew the exact details of her half brother's actions.

Swandra's face vanished from the mirror. "I don't think it matters now, and you couldn't prove anything I'm saying, not that you would. I see you as someone who would not tattle."

Swandra's head, a moon dodging in and out of the clouds, appeared again. "Heidi was hiding my half brother in the storage room and I went to talk to him, to urge him to help us."

"Please don't tug my hair for saying it," Eleanor responded, "but this mumbo jumbo about the Shakespeare folio is not credible. Kugelmann was in jail for months. Surely, he would have told a trusted lawyer about the folio so the Serbs could go and retrieve it. No, I think you wanted to get him to kill Mary, who had stolen your sweetheart just like the baron stole your half brother's."

Swandra dropped the comb. "What an idea. If anyone wanted him to commit an atrocity, it was Heidi and her fanatic friends. But even she had to curb her blood lust."

She stooped to get the comb as Eleanor asked, "What was stopping her?"

"From what I heard, they needed your damn Shakespeare. They had ransacked the Feckleses' house when the couple were away. They didn't find it. The folio was stashed somewhere."

"Why did they break out your half brother if they didn't need him?" Eleanor asked.

"From what I heard, they had just found out about the millionaire getting the book and had to change all their plans." It was as if Swandra couldn't locate the comb, because she remained crouched on the floor.

Eleanor looked into her own eyes reflectively. "It sounds like I'm trying to find you out," she told Swandra. "Or find the Serbs out. That's not the point. You know I'm in full sympathy with the Serbian independence movement. I got interested in the murder because our friend Dr. Cranky was falsely arrested."

Eleanor stopped. It was disconcerting to talk to someone who was sitting on the floor. She continued, "Cranky is free now, but I've continued looking into things because, well, I think every murder is a parable, *n'est-ce pas*? Even if the Serbian independence movement isn't directly involved, it did supply the conditions."

"How do you mean?" Swandra said from the floor.

Glancing back, Eleanor saw the maid was sitting on a stool.

"Well, it's a prejudice I have. People say the brickwork of society—the food, the clothes, the amenities—are due to people's labor, whether it's making beds, tending looms, handing out punch at a soiree—creating things and adding surplus value.

"But if you look at it, there are things beneath that, underground watercourses, the people's social movements, ones which are sometimes on the surface, like the Serbian independence fight or labor organizing in the Midlands. These people's currents are what influence and direct events. And it's the ferocity of the struggle that shapes what will happen.

"Doesn't the way these murders were framed by the Serbian battle for autonomy prove this? It's a prejudice of mine."

Eleanor became quiet, listening, and then Swandra spoke from her low perch. "I heard they now wanted Erick to steal the book. They said he had nothing to lose. That's why I had to see him. I told him to ignore them, that what he should do is run to America."

Eleanor asked timidly, "Did he agree with you?" She was thinking, wildly, maybe the radical Serbs murdered him with poison when he refused their plans.

"It wasn't decided," Swandra said. "Nothing is ever decided."

As she concluded, she stood up again and glanced across Eleanor's shoulder at the glass. Both were silent, looking into each other's eyes, at first remove.

Chapter 12

Cranky was coming back from his early promenade, headed for his room in the hotel, when he was met by a bellhop from the Hotel Pupp, who told him he was wanted in the rooms of Mary Van Winkle.

It so happened that a pretty little maid from the hotel was temporarily in Mary's employ. Cranky had only spoken to her once, when she was serving canapés at a little get-to-gether. Evidently, he had left quite the impression. So, Cranky imagined, with her mistress in jail, the maid was probably taking the opportunity to summon him.

He and the bellhop entered the lavish Pupp, ascended the staircase, and were let into Mary's apartment, though not by the maid Cranky had hoped to see. He was left to wait in the drawing room.

The room was large and watched over by a portrait, which took up a whole wall, of Emperor Franz Joseph in a white military costume sprinkled with medals and cut by a red-trimmed white sash. His full beard and sideburns were so profuse they blocked much of his face.

It was not the picture, though, so much as its grandiose setting that caught one's attention. The big wall had one large portion painted light blue, against the cream coloring of the rest of the apartment. Inside this frame were painted baroque streamers arranged in a rectangular pattern. The painting was at the bull's-eye of these overlapping frames.

This was not the only unusual feature of the room. The furnishings were in the late Empire style, with a number of low, backless couches, more for reclining on than sitting; chairs sparsely backed with two thin verticals and a single cross piece; and two or three oval tables. However, as if a dance recital were about to take place, everything had been pushed back to the walls, leaving only two chairs sitting, as if forgotten, in the center of the space.

The door of the side room flew open, and a woman came out, saying, as she saw Cranky, "You still owe us fifty pounds."

The speaker was Mary Van Winkle.

Once Cranky had gotten over the shocks of Mary's being free and of her abrupt demand for funds, he was further discomfited by her dress, which was a riding costume. She had on a short dark skirt, without bustle, and a crimson blouse with the brightness of a lighthouse.

She charged onward. "Buck up, old charger. You stare at me like I just stepped out of the tomb, or should I say New York's Tombs prison? Would that be more accurate?"

Cranky, near overwhelmed, said, "I thought you were incarcerated."

"That Hubner is no four-flusher. He said if there really was a masked villain, as you testified, the police should be able to find a trace, a bloody mask or something."

"And?" Cranky asked, feeling his way on shifting ground.

"They found the *something*, a blood-encrusted knife concealed in a back shed."

"I never thought you killed your husband," he said.

"I'd be more likely to kill my maid, or she me for that matter," Mary replied.

"Why would she do that?" Cranky asked. Perplexities seemed to increase rather than diminish with each new explanation.

"Molly's been in a four-year huff ever since the Versailles stink."

"I'm lost," Cranky said.

"I sank; I sank," Mary said, for the first time admitting weakness. "I joined the gauntlet in Versailles to spit on these traitors. So shameful."

"How is that shameful?" he asked.

"To squeeze in among a vile crowd, even if a crowd of my betters, is lowering yourself. She never got over it."

"The maid?"

"Molly. She was so outraged by my going into the street, into the maelstrom. She's hated me since. If her Communard comrades made up a subscription to kill me or my husband, she's donated the largest amount."

"I'm still lost," he told her. "How was your deceased husband involved in this?"

"They blame him for selling bayonets to the Prussians. They're all half-cracked. It's the simple law of supply and demand. Try explaining economics to Molly or that sway-backed Swandra, her *bosom* friend. They got together on Molly's day off, for what type of unnatural playtime I don't care to speculate."

"How does Swandra enter in?"

"During the Commune war, she was the maid in a Serbian family that had come to Versailles. The family also joined the gauntlet. There was a row and Swandra quit. Molly never quit. I'll give that to her."

Cranky was thinking. What if the hot-tempered Mary had gotten into a dispute with Molly and impulsively stabbed her? Or the two got into a dispute, Molly wielding the knife, but the maid fell on the blade herself? Although Mary hadn't offered the police any plausible explanation of what had happened, that could be because she had totally lost her head and didn't know how to explain herself. Through a mix of very bad fortune and luck, there was another killer in the wings who did away with her husband. This was devastating to Mary, Cranky thought, but it did cover over her own murder, which could be attributed to the criminal who knifed her husband, pulling out a second blade rather than use the one that was left in Molly.

Mary conducted Cranky to the chairs that sat dead center in the room. As he was seating himself, he noticed the maid he had spoken to was standing at the hotel corridor entrance to the room while a second maid attended the door to the inner apartments. They were like sentries.

The peculiar furniture arrangement, which left them as isolated as an iceberg that had drifted too far south, was hard to explain. Cranky wondered if it were due to some concern of Mary's for privacy, not wanting to let the maids overhear anything, but the woman's braying voice seemed to preclude that. Maybe she just had an odd sense of theatricality.

He took up her earlier remark. "If the police found the tainted knife, that means there was a second bladesman besides the one who killed Molly. Or perhaps Molly's killer was concealed when you entered. But how would this villain know you were going to the pump room that early?"

"Dear lubber," Mary said, "the long of it is, the hotel staff knew we were getting up early to go to the pump room. We asked at the desk if they would open the room early. That request was pigeonholed. And at dinner the night before, Henry spoke of it at table, surrounded by knowing heads. In sum, half the Pupp knew or might have known. I'm sorry I didn't put it in the newspaper so you might have read about it.

"But to talk about the murders is hardly the reason I summoned you here. You owed a debt to Henry. I don't need it all, but right now, with the death fouling up my finances, I'm caught short. I need money pronto."

Her voice had dropped a few octaves, and he could see why she wouldn't want her scandalous demands made public by back-hall gossip.

"Madam," Cranky said, "your husband is barely cold."

"I sound a bit rapacious, don't I, Farebrother? But you see, I want to try a run at the tables."

Worse and worse, Cranky thought.

She hitched her chair closer to his, so their knees nearly abutted.

"I know it's a mania," she told him. "And it's almost a tradition. When the love of my life, the Kentucky colonel, died, died on the field of honor battling those Union Yankees, I sold up what was left of my plantation and gamed it away.

"This new bird didn't just repair my fortunes, he reformed me. Or almost. Once we were married, I forswore all games of chance. But now—"

Cranky thought that it was strange to hear a woman, or anyone for that matter, unbutton to a stranger, even in trying to create sympathy to raise funds. He remembered Americans were known for their inability to censor themselves.

"I want to get to the casino," she went on, "and need some money, quick, quick."

"Which you will lose," Cranky said with a trace of melancholy that was not only outer-directed but, as he could see, touched also on his own ineffectual summer romances.

"I won't lose it," she told him. Mary's complexion seemed to have grown lighter, like a crystal glass pushed into a stem of light. "I've hit on a sharpie—what's his name, Prick-the-Dome or something—and he will help me build a few assets while I'm waiting for my legacy."

"I can get you some money," Cranky said, speaking with little certainty.

"I'll see you when I return," she said, pushing back her chair, and started to turn away.

"But where are you going?"

"I'll be riding up to the Freudenberg castle. I believe a clue to my husband's death is to be found there."

"What kind of clue could be found there?" he pressed.

"You know I'm a book collector. I bought one of your volumes. I found out the Freudenbergs had a lost folio of Shakespeare, which passed from them to Kugelmann to Feckles. My husband was negotiating—damn the price—to obtain it for me."

Mary stood in front of Cranky and placed her hands firmly on his shoulders, pulling up so he felt obligated to stand. She shifted, her hands still guiding, so he was turned to the door.

Speaking with that same coldness, Mary said, "I will find my husband's killer. Aha. No doubt on that score."

An icy feeling crept up Cranky's spine. It wasn't because of her allusion to riding on her fool's errand or the mysterious book. It was her "Aha," which he recognized as an abbreviation of her late husband's "Aha-ha."

Chapter 13

For breakfast, Eleanor had egg dumplings and sausage. Marx, on short rations, had a mushroom soufflé, onions on the side, and black coffee. Then her father said, "Let's step outside, Empress. Perhaps I might permit myself one cheroot. I'm due for the full treatment today at the baths."

The hotel was set back from the main avenue by an envelope of greensward cut by a flagged walkway. The two walked down to the street, where they stopped to watch the passing throng of strollers, riders, and carriages. Marx lit his cigar and brought up something that was worrying him.

"The lad Sherlock has a prying look, as if he's suspected I'm not Herr Arbuthnot."

"Stuff and nonsense, dear Papa. The boy's head is filled with crime and detecting the facts, his hard facts, behind the Van Winkle murders."

Marx choked on a large puff, spilling some ash on his beard, which he had to brush out with his fingers. He went on, "That is what I'm worried about. He suspects everyone. He's like a mad fisherman who casts his nets on the water, on the sand, on a reef."

Eleanor clapped her hands. "Look, Father, what a beautiful equipage."

She was calling his attention to a lovely closed black and gold carriage that was approaching. The overall body was black, set off with gold highlight stripes and a golden crest. There were sparkling glass windows on the doors and in the front. Unlit lanterns on poles in either front corner resembled the streetlights of Vienna. It rode high on over-large wheels and was pulled by four sturdy roans.

All this showed a refined taste absent from the next coach in line. This one resembled an art gallery on wheels. On the sides were images of lyre-strumming angels. Above the doors, in a meteorological fantasy, were clouds mixed with floating, grape-laden vines. In the very center of the cloud drifts was another angel who had chosen just that spot to indite a poem. The wheels and trimming were gold leaf, as were markings on the mixed red and gold lamps lifted at each corner of the body. On the top was a big red button, as if the carriage were a large, rolling pound cake that needed a cherry on top. The coach was drawn by four magnificent white stallions. They were a good match for the white-haired dowager who hung out the window.

"Father, look who's coming," Eleanor said, pointing to another sight. "Here comes Von Pelt. See how well he sits his mount."

He was splendid in his green topcoat, short in front with a tail in back and a double row of brass buttons that sparkled as if they were winking at her. He had cream-colored pants and leather boots, and around his neck was a mass of white ruffles that resembled the spume of a churning stream.

He was on a roan mare, its overall light-brown coloring sometimes overwhelmed by the mixed-in white hairs, which broke through altogether to form a patch on its forehead.

It seemed to Eleanor that he was about to doff his hat to her when instead he looked behind, hearing another steed coming up at a gallop. The poor horse was then reined back with such force it almost lost its teeth. Mary Van Winkle was the rider.

Chapter 14

Seeing Mary Van Winkle out of jail might have engrossed Marx's attention if he hadn't been preoccupied with his health. While sick people in hospitals got bed sores from lying too long in one position, Marx was having similar skin problems—carbuncles, cysts, and indentations—from long hours sitting. Work, eating, drinking—all the things one did in living—were ruining his health. Not work, of course, but overwork. Yet how let up when the demands on his time (back at home base in London) were so unavoidable: *Capital 2*, translations of *1*, political meetings for the unions and socialists, correspondence, family upsets such as Laura's marriage, Eleanor's flirtation with an older man, and money needs, always money needs? Not eating so much as overeating. But how turn down a friend, such as his English translator Sam Moore, who might invite him for a repast after a town hall, or how not eat when a Christmas goose appeared out of season, plump and hearty, courtesy of Engels? Not drinking regularly but occasionally long bouts, at a table of good fellowship, partaking of the highly palatable English stout, or wine, or the whiskey Engels liked to occasionally swim about in.

At this point he was relying on Feckles's regime, which entailed keeping to the diet, morning and evening constitutionals, and daily snoutfuls, which mounted up, starting with one daily glass, going up to twenty per diem. That was quite an intake, although nothing compared to that of an American woman, whom, Eleanor reported on in a letter to Laura, "said she was in a hurry, so at one sitting downed 4 gallons. Father remarked if she had been drinking brandy, it would have killed her."

Marx arrived at the spa facility. After exchanging his clothes for a large bath towel, he entered a shower stall. Hooking the cloth on a peg, he allowed his heavy body to luxuriate under the pallidly warm water. When fully wetted, he redonned his towel and followed a party of similarly attired gentlemen to the hot-air vault. This was a narrow, tiled room; long benches ran along the wall, a skylight letting in enough light to read by. One other bench, "the pew," ran down the center.

The air was a trifle warmer than outside, but the place was part of the acclimatization process. In the way mountain climbers will pause at way stations, allowing them to grow accustomed to thinner air, so in "balneotherapy," patients moved slowly up, and then later down, a gradient leading to and away from the hottest rooms.

Marx never knew what company he was going to keep when he started a treatment regimen. At times, among the patients there was a general conversation, often about the current political clime or the Viennese opera season. Other times, everyone had fallen down into himself, so Marx, too, would stay silent, joining the general brood.

Today he saw that two fellows seated on the back shelf had laced up their towels like togas. He took a seat on the pew. Beside him sat a stilted young man, Pricklestone, rumored to be a flimflammer. The bloke held a newspaper in his hands, which he had to keep straightening as if propping up a wilting flower.

As no conversation was going on, Marx began thinking about the Serbian independence movement. He had a theory that the Serbians were pursuing a lost cause. Vigorous nations, whether presently prosperous, like Germany, or temporarily weakened, like Italy, someday would play a large part on the global stage. But others, such as Serbia, would never gain a place in the world historical footlights.

Hegel, the philosopher who had reigned as supreme authority during Marx's youth, believed lack of historical significance was due to ethnic temperament. He believed the Chinese were locked into an overly reverent attitude toward the emperor and, indeed, any paternal authority and so could not arrive at a progressive individuality. But Marx, more in line with Montesquieu, felt a nation's weakness derived from geography and history. If a country wanted to prosper, it had to (1) have resources to utilize or, at least, have easy access to them, as England had its coal and colonies; (2) have a population to exploit, such as the displaced peasants of Britain, driven from their farms by landlords who wanted fields to raise sheep and hunt foxes; and, lastly, (3) have a good quality of exploiter, such as the English bourgeoisie and feudal squires, who could work in tandem to marshal resources for an industrial takeoff.

But Serbia lacked all three things: (3) it was blocked because its nobility had refeudalized, forcing its peasants back into serfdom to produce not for the estate but for export crops, so the prices they obtained rose and fell on the world market, making the landlords weak sisters and not likely to power industrialization; (2) the refeudalization kept the serfs land-tied; and (1) the associated Hungarian-Austrian-German extractors siphoned off the silver, coal, and wood, so there were no resources to use internally.

Only remnants—intellectuals, small tradesmen, maids, professionals, and dissident nobility—pushed for change, which was resisted by the massive force of the system as a whole.

Marx glanced back at the stilted fellow. Due to the moisture, his journal had now crumpled into wastepaper.

Marx knew that a room by its contours either propped up or discouraged talk. As soon as time was called and they all proceeded to the sauna, they found themselves in a more congenial atmosphere. Pricklestone dropped any pretense of examining his soggy news sheet, which, even if crisp, would have served little purpose in the dimly lit sauna, where the bracing heat was swelling up from the grate. The newspaper reader brought up the celebrated topic of the moment. "The millionaire's wife has been sprung from the trap," he began. "No one knows why."

He was one of those hound-faced characters with a disproportionally long nose and eyes set wide apart as if they were recoiling from it. His whiskers were trimmed down so the full contour of his chin and cheeks was visible. His body was lean and tightly muscled.

He had turned to Marx with his remark as they both sat akimbo on the bottom bench. From behind them on the second, higher bench, someone commented, "One knows why."

Marx glanced back. Wrapped up in a towel was Sergeant Hubner, whom he hadn't noticed.

"Dear Sergeant, I didn't recognize you in all this steam."

Marx hadn't expected to exchange further words with these two—a thief and a thief taker—and when he did, he saw it as a product of their place. Chumminess of the kind experienced by the rich at their gentlemen's clubs and the poor in pubs also appeared in a shared sauna.

They sat in a small box, the door and coal grate on one side where a porthole let in a trickle of tinged light. There was an L of seats on an upper and lower rank on which the men squeezed together, sweating, near naked. Two in the back corner had undraped altogether, Greek style. This situation brought about an unforced intimacy. After all, the silk waistcoats, stickpins, collars, and top hats, if any possessed them, accoutrements that signaled social rank, were missing, and every man, as far as they were strangers, unless he introduced himself, was only an envelope of flesh.

"I see you didn't notice me," Hubner responded, "but I recognized you in both your identities: as Dr. Arbuthnot and Herr Marx."

With that, Marx's house of cards tumbled to the ground. He had deluded himself into thinking the police authorities had overlooked his presence. But why they had waited this long to let him know they were watching him? Moreover, he thought, if Hubner knew, then probably the boy Sherlock, who was dogging the policeman's steps, must also know.

Marx glanced over at his companion, now privy to his identity, seeing how he was taking it. He was annoyed, to say the least, by this unexpected exposure, and then surprised when he saw his benchmate seemed even more discomposed than Marx was himself. Judging by his face, he would have been visibly sweating if he wasn't already. Now this fellow faced stolidly forward, not even turning back to the policeman when he commented, "You've proven yourself."

"I can go further," Hubner said, "you are Jacob Pricklestone, a notorious con player who recently slipped the British net and have come here, undoubtedly hoping to work a scheme on Van Winkle."

"So, you know everything," said Pricklestone glumly.

The Czechs went on talking obliviously. Then one got up and, saying in Italian, "*Permettimi di*," took up a ladle that was swung over a water bucket, dipped it in, and sprinkled its contents over the thickly laid coals, producing a rush of curdling steam, which hit the front-row sitters with a splash of hot foam, at first stinging but then ebbing into a satisfying, bone-penetrating warmth. Everyone luxuriated for a time as the sweat poured streamers from their hairlines and beards and marked wet furrows down their chests. Conversation lay low for a few minutes, and then there was a clip on the door from the attendant. It was time to go downslope to the vapor baths.

Pricklestone excused himself, saying he was ending his treatment for the day, as he had affairs to which he had to attend. This left Hubner and Marx to proceed to the next station, the vapor bath.

In size, it was midway between the sauna and the hot-air room. Like the second location, it had wall benches and a couple of pews in the middle. There was a tang to the air, for it had been treated with special salts and minerals, their savors concealed under a sheen of lavender oil.

Marx had never had a long conversation with a policeman, but he would like to know if he would have any problems now that the man knew his identity. He wasn't sure how to ask. Marx referred to Pricklestone: "A man like that. He seems to have no principles."

Hubner asked, "Have you read E.T.A. Hoffmann?"

"We all read him when we were young."

Hubner went on, "Do you know what our great master Goethe said about Hoffmann?"

"I don't."

"He said Hoffmann is dreadfully amusing on the surface, but if you allow yourself to look deeper, your judgment would have to be, 'Sick, sick, sick.'"

"Why would he say that?"

"Because Hoffmann saw into man's second half," Hubner said sententiously.

"And what might that be?"

"Every person has two selves: one for normal, everyday use, and the other a concealed, evil half, ready to break out at any time."

Marx commented, "You are giving me an idea as old as Platonism, in which each human has two elements, the charioteer of reason that must hold in check the horses of passion."

Hubner turned excitedly to Marx, seemingly more passionate about this than police work. "Hoffmann is not talking of a divided consciousness pulled this way and that. He is talking of two complete consciousnesses."

Marx was thinking, *Hubner is just another dummkopf.* He commented, "This sounds like pseudo-Hegelian nonsense."

Even more worked up, Hubner continued, "Do you know Hoffmann's 'The Mines of Falun'? No? Let me sketch it in. In this short story, he presents this idea of the two distinct minds in marvelous symbolic garb. Here's how it goes.

"A young man comes to the mining district wondering if working underground is his vocation. However, he is scared off by the noxious stink and dirt of the workings. He makes to leave when he spies the beauteous daughter of the head foreman and goes head over heels. He immediately gets a job as a pickman."

"What are you getting at?" Marx interrogated.

"Now things change. He begins to show two totally different personalities, depending on what side of the earth he inhabits. On the surface, he is a practical, slow-moving, bashful swain. Once he goes under the soil to his workplace, he changes. Now he is a bold adventurer, leading the other men to the richest veins and savagely attacking the walls of coal. He is now forceful, aggressive, almost untamed. And Hoffmann, with his metaphysical side, shows that the hero's reaction when he is in the pit is due to his becoming attuned to the mystic tenor of the *elementals*, the secret souls of gems and minerals."

Marx said, a bit scornfully, "Sounds as if the clouds have descended into the coal mines so the hero can poke his head into them."

"Friend, you are missing the *symbolic* significance whose truth I see every moment in my police work."

Marx said fretfully, "I understand that, in your reading, criminals are those who have fallen in with these dark elementals, though I fail to see what practical application this doctrine might have."

Hubner defended his idea. "It has helped me understand myself. With my lower self, I chase criminals, perhaps I slip into their haunts, and as I spy on them, I drink the hard, poisonous swill they favor. But then when I am home, inhabiting my higher self, I sit in my chamber imbibing another beverage. I taste draughts of Schiller and Novalis—"

His listing of the German giants of poetry was cut short by an outpouring of steam, a long one, making it seem for a moment as if the room were providing an artificial cloud cover, the one Marx imagined invading the mines, or perhaps as if they were on a Wagnerian stage in the midst of a smoky scene of battle as a city was being overturned.

Further names by the officer were stopped by a loud rap on the door, indicating time was up. So the two got up, each going off to a separate stall for a mixed shower, followed by a rubdown.

The mixed shower was a Karlsbad novelty, an alternating flow of warm and cool water, which, it was said, "creates a relaxing rhythm that will gradually lift the body down from the rigors of the sauna's stoked heat."

After that experience, Marx walked, towel-swathed, into the next room, an alcove where there was a masseuse at the ready. Preparing to lie down, he noticed to his surprise that among the toiletries, salves, creams, and oils was a crib book of Hegel. He would have been less surprised if he saw a Black Forest elf peeping from the towel hamper.

He took up the book for a moment, then said, "You have the look of a university student," as he set his head into the indentation on the massage table.

"That I am, sir," said the youth. In appearance, he was short and slack muscled, but he provided a vigorous rubdown, starting on the back and shoulders, standing above Marx's head. At first, he kept to one place, pushing down repeatedly on a frame of muscles. Then he began a longer stroke, moving down the back and along either side of the spine with a soothing, smoothing stroke. Once done there, he came around, stopping halfway down, and attacked the same expanse of back from another angle.

Sinking into a relaxed calm, Marx asked, "Where are you studying?"

The boy replied, "Karlsbad is my summer school, Berlin my fall and winter study post. Master Trove at your service."

"And you take up philosophy?"

"Everything can be explained by Hegel." That thought seemed to infuse him with energy, since it was accompanied by a series of short, hard strokes down Marx's back. "He is unjustly neglected at present, a situation not fated to last." Now the fellow took up one of Marx's arms, pulling the skin as if to pinch it.

Marx was no slouch when it came to Hegel, but rather than offering his own thoughts, he was content to overhear the young man's musings. He prodded Trove a little, as he was being prodded from the other side, the student having walked around to the other arm. "Since you claim your Hegel is the see-all and end-all of thought, how would he apply himself to solving the Van Winkle murder case?"

Now the boy was working Marx's fingers, giving each one a steady pressure followed by a sudden snap so the knuckles popped. He said, "It's simple: the slave and master exterminated each other."

"And then?"

"I know you are a professor, Dr. Arbuthnot. Do you know the *Phenomenology*?" the youth asked. He had gone over to Marx's legs, stroking down from the thighs. "The lordship-bondage chapter, how does that read?"

Marx told the boy, "Hegel says the slave fears death and that's why he lets himself be captured. The master, a true Greek, would rather die in battle than fall into someone's hands."

Trove's strokes weakened in intensity as he monitored Marx's description.

"According to the philosopher, the slave, forced to labor with his hands—making things, tables, pianos, nudging things to grow—learns how the world works and how he can work with it, guiding it effectively. The master in his castle controls but has lost the ability to interact. So, we end with a savvy, wily bondsman and a powerful but intellectually starved lord."

Marx finished, turning over so his front could get a rubdown. Trove began soaping his hand, saying, "You see my point?"

Marx chuckled. "If it's to give me a good massage, yes; if it's to explain the murders, no."

Standing and looking down as soap dripped on Marx's chest, the youth put it like this: "I would go beyond Hegel to say that as the slave learns, he chafes more and more, because he realizes he is being held down by his inferior. This leads to revolt, the revolt Hegel praised in the slave rising in Haiti. There comes a bursting point. The maid couldn't swallow her pride any longer and had to revolt."

Trove was so enthusiastic that he splashed some soap in Marx's face, then apologized. The masseuse cleaned off his face and, in the final process, washed him down. As he was being cleaned off, Marx looked at the highly varnished flat side of the table holding the notions and saw a muddied reflection of his own image, making him look, with his pot and quite hairy torso, like the wolf man that was said to have done away with Van Winkle.

Marx went off to a second mixed shower, but not before leaving a tip for Trove, who stayed silent, approvingly silent. From there it was on to the heated pool, where, after exchanging towel for trunks, he entered the coed facility, which was a good deal livelier than his previous stations.

The pool had three lanes: two for swimming—mainly,

slow paddling—and one in which people could congregate. It was a long oblong of a room, with a set of high windows along one side that let in a wave of strong sun that lit the penciled blue dolphins and sea nymphs decorating the white walls.

As he entered, Marx saw the lieutenant was braking at lane's end to make a turn as he swam lengths. Marx waded down the steps and strode past the chatting patients, making for the deeper water. He passed Mrs. Smallweed and two lady friends who were hanging on the rim, letting their bodies float out behind them so that in their green and blue bathing costumes they resembled water plants drifting on a quiet stream. He took his own place on the edge, up to his armpits in the lukewarm liquid.

Left alone in the sonic mix of lapping water and overlapping conversations, Marx closed his eyes, feeling relaxed, reassured that though his identity was known to the police, it would not lead to any repercussions in their remaining few days here. Nothing would happen even if, as he suspected, Sherlock had found out Marx's true name from Hubner and badgered the policeman about taking some sort of action.

As he was buoyed by the water, which held him in its width, he thought a moment of his student days in Bonn, led backward by Hubner's mention of Hoffmann. The tale the policeman brought up, "The Mines of Falun," a piece Marx didn't know, revealed an interesting side to Hoffmann. His most-known pieces, such as "The Sandman" and "The Golden Flowerpot," were centered on a hero who was splayed between two women: one a domestic, housewife sort and the other an exotic temptress, perhaps, as in "Sandman," a super-sensual Italian, who had ties to chthonic depths.

But in "Falun," the contrast had changed and had become that between the everyday and workaday worlds.

This hinted Hoffmann was finding his way to probe something fundamental. Some of his plots, the love intrigues and murders, showed an awareness of society's bottommost forces, labor and slavery.

As he thought this over, Marx nodded, allowing the sound of talk to become barely audible as he wandered into a half sleep, the water in its motion almost rhythmic, imparting the gentle rocking of a train carriage.

He was aroused from his reverie by an attendant ringing a cowbell to signal the end of the session. He waded to the end of the pool, reflecting that the "Falun" story gave him new respect for Hoffmann, whom he had previously thought of as little more than a punter.

As Marx tramped off to the sprudel room, Hubner fell in beside him.

This smaller basin was not for swimming but for rejuvenation. People stood in the low water or sat, their head and shoulders above water, in marble seats that extended underwater along the sides. Through the sand underfoot, naturally carbonated water was festively bubbling up, giving the pool the effervescence of a volcanic lake.

The two went to stand in the pool, ranging themselves toward the center, where they wouldn't be overheard. In any case, fewer and fewer people were around. Many had doctors who recommended only certain parts of the regimen. Others were too eager to get back to the social swirl to stick out the whole course of treatment.

Marx ventured, "You brought up that Pricklestone was scheming to bilk old Van Winkle, but I heard the old codger was terribly stingy. I don't see how this dummkopf Pricklestone could siphon any off."

"First he had to seduce the wife," Marx was informed.

Feeling the same gentle lassitude he felt in the heated pool, Marx decided to rest on the undersea chair, hoping he wasn't going to be splashed in his face by a passing bather.

"You mean seduce the woman? He hardly seems a ladies' man," Marx commented.

Slowly lowering himself so they were at the same level, Hubner said, "Through his cat's-paw, Pricklestone wanted to seduce Mary to play at the casino, which her husband had forbidden."

"Not easy of accomplishment," Marx returned, watching the bubbles popping on the surface as if fish were surrounding him.

"The man is well organized. Von Pelt is in his pay."

A dropsical fellow and chubby companion lumbered by, sending out a wake that doused Marx to the chin. After spitting water, he said, "So this Von Pelt is also one of your double-faced characters?"

"Yes, but you see, in him, you have to take it differently. His higher nature has been corrupted. His military virtues, his savoir-faire, all those sterling traits are used for bad ends."

"Your psychology is getting a bit slippery," Marx told him. "You told me before that a man has two separate personalities, one usually submerged. They are like a business suit and evening clothes. But now, a further split. Each of the two personalities can incline to good or evil. I think there's a much simpler explanation for someone like Von Pelt."

"Be careful now," Hubner warned as he stood up. He was indicating a meaty cleric who had just waded into the pool center and kept dunking himself and then relaunching himself into the air. Once he resurfaced, the water flew off him as if he were a breaching whale and cast waves in their direction.

Marx continued, "You must have seen how these hotel servants bow and fawn over all the haughty moneybags they are assigned to care for. You can guess they are angry about losing their dignity catering to the whims of the wealthy. That breeds resentment and, perhaps, the urge to betray them. That could account for Von Pelt's joining forces with Pricklestone and so elevating his underground self."

"There's some sense in that," Hubner conceded. "The poor always envy those who have rank and noble bearing. That's why they seldom honor the natural aristocrats, I mean, the poets of greatness. That's why these Serbs always complain they are oppressed by Austria-Hungary. They belong to an inferior race, an envious group, a people that is too spiritless to craft their own state, and are fated to live as vassals."

Marx felt uneasily that he had voiced a like opinion, which seemed much less plausible coming from this dummkopf.

Warming to his theme, Hubner continued, "We Germans have the principles of a fully formed race. We know our station. We look neither above nor below but straightfor- wardly ahead, where our duty lies. Whatever your politics, Herr Marx, as a German you must agree."

"I daresay," Marx said, and nodded. "Even yet, I wonder if even your beloved Hoffmann does not *in symbolic garb* suggest an approval of this same burning class envy."

"That's absurd."

"Yet it was you yourself, Herr Hubner, who suggested as much," Marx said, needling him.

"What do you mean?" Hubner asked.

"You mentioned that the young miner in 'Falun' happened to possess two souls. One, seen above ground, was that of a genial, domesticated homebody, but below ground, he was savage and driven. But could his below- ground self be motivated by envy transmuted into coiled rage?"

"But what would he have to envy?" Hubner asked.

"It's not like the spite borne by a servant who has the object of her anger in front of her. The miner of Hoffmann is angry at a process. Mining had been a noble handicraft of lodge brothers, but the advancement of civilization, with the mines taken over by big capitalist firms, the German firms, meant the death of the crafts. What was left was industrial drudgery. Naturally, he was enraged, but he showed it in a displaced way."

"I should have expected such a line from you, Herr Marx," Hubner broke out angrily. "It is such ideas that are used to justify strikes, pillaging, and any villainy. A man like Pricklestone will use them. He'll say to himself, 'I could have been a lawyer or journalist, but due to poverty, I couldn't go to school and attain the heights my abilities merited, so instead I'll fill up with anger and become a blackguard and killer.'"

"Killer?" Marx echoed.

"I'm letting my thinking go to extremes, but one wonders how desperate he is. He is trying to coax the wife, Mary, to go to the casino, but she balks because her crusty old husband forbids it. So why not eliminate the old bird?"

"Any evidence?" Marx said, fascinated by this turn of the subject.

"One strand, but it's hardly much. A patrolman saw him lurking around the pump room around midnight on the night before the murders," Hubner said.

"That doesn't make sense," Marx said. "Why would he sneak a look at the pump room when he could visit it during the day?"

Hubner added, "It's not clear the pump room was his object. He may have had a second scheme on hand."

"Such as?"

Hubner leaned back as a flap of water hit them. He continued, "Maybe he was looking over the Feckleses' apartment, from which he thought of stealing a folio."

"How's that?" Marx said, feigning surprise. He had already heard something about this folio over breakfast, when Eleanor had mentioned it.

"It is rumored that Kugelmann had passed a valuable Shakespeare folio to Dr. Feckles, who was supposed to sell it to get funds to serve the Serbian cause. But it turns out the good doctor kept it for himself. Or had it until now. Another rumor has it that he sold it to old Van Winkle."

Marx nodded, noting this new point, as Feckles continued. "There's another curious point. I asked Dr. Feckles, who came home late that night, if he had noticed anything untoward. Wouldn't he have seen Pricklestone in a doorway across from his house?"

"That's understandable," Marx commented. "The doctor must have been tired."

"I happened to check with the stableman, who told me Dr. Feckles brought in his horse at ten p.m. Yet as he testified, as I learned from other sources, he didn't cross his own threshold till midnight. So where did he get off to?"

Marx shifted back to the original point. "As to Pricklestone, I don't see him as a killer. A swindler, yes; a dummkopf, yes; an assassin, no."

"These types are hard to characterize," Hubner said.

Marx gave his idea. "I think criminals are specialists, the piece workers Adam Smith raves about. Each man keeps to his line—their station, as you would say."

"Pricklestone's expertise is cards."

"What exactly does he do?" Marx asked.

"Let me show you," Hubner said, wading out a little to stand facing Marx, who also stood. "Once they got Mary Van Winkle to the casino, she would play baccarat."

"I don't know it."

"Not a gambler, eh? It's simple enough. You play against the dealer, trying to reach twenty-one. Face cards count ten. If you exceed the twenty-one, you lose. Imagine I'm dealing. Each time I ripple the water toward you, it's a card traveling into your hand." He sent a small wavelet in Marx's direction. "So, what do you have?"

Marx was willing to play along; after all, didn't his daughters often rope him into playing charades? "A king."

"That's ten. Do you want a second?"

"Of course, this is short."

Another wave pushed out from Hubner's cupped palm. "And now?"

"A jack."

"That's twenty."

"Stand pat."

"Good choice. Now Mary's playing against the dealer, who would have to be in the pay of this trio, and also against another cardsman, who would be Pricklestone. Suppose a card went to you, Mary, and then, with a second gesture ..." Hubner sent one fuller, one lesser lip of water forward, but this second, smaller wave was checked by a heavy flow of water coming from the bouncing abbot.

"Yes," Hubner said, nodding his head. "This proves"—he meant the way his wave had been crushed—"it's easy for things to go wrong."

On the side of the pool, a clapper appeared, bringing their session, the last of the series, to an end. The two trailed back toward the pool steps and said adieus, each going to the shower stalls. Marx scrubbed up, redonned his clothes, checked his hair and beard, and issued back into the town.

As he walked back, Marx began assimilating two registers of information, both literary. There was Hoffmann's idea of the two-parted individual *and* there was the stolen folio, which it seemed Van Winkle might have had among his possessions.

Could that mean the Serbian movement had also become two-faced in its strategy, one side desiring to kill Van Winkle through an anarchist "attendant," which would show the rich that if they dabbled in repressing the Serbs they might die at a martyr's hands, and the other side wanting to leave him alive and steal the book from him?

He looked at this idea from a number of perspectives. One thing he liked to do when assessing a problem was to form a combinatorial diagram, putting all the possibilities in a set of boxes. But that wouldn't work here. Another way to look at things, one he borrowed from Hegel, was to ascend to wider and wider generalities.

He walked slowly past the Bohemian buildings, all festooned in bright pinks, hazels, and yellows, so bright you'd suspect fairies came out each night to paint them afresh, and considered this method, which might be vulgarly called "drop down, drop down."

There were two sets of crimes: the murder of Van Winkle and the maid and the poisoning of Kugelmann. Common sense, the policemen's first view of things, was these were unconnected cases, but public opinion, which Sherlock claimed always pointed in the right direction, saw a link. Kugelmann stumbled into the pump room and, him being the newspaper stereotype of "a fiend in human shape," slaughtered master and maid just so they couldn't reveal his whereabouts.

The public was right in seeing a connection, but they had imagined what happened in terms of a penny dreadful plot. To really see the links, one had to ... *drop down, drop down*.

The actual tie between the crimes was (it seemed) the Serbian independence movement to which Kugelmann belonged and to which Van Winkle was also attached, both because he had something they wanted, the folio, and because he had done something they detested, supply weapons to Austrian oppressors. Still, relying on this pattern to interpret events left something still unexplained.

Drop down, drop down.

From the newspapers, Marx had learned that Molly was in Versailles during the Paris Commune uprising. He had also heard the rumor that there were a number of ex-Communards forming an association in Karlsbad. This group must know that Van Winkle supplied the Prussians who had helped slaughter their fellows during the uprising. Could they also have known, through Molly, of the existence of the folio?

Marx then said to himself, "Let's say as a hypothesis that money was uppermost. Then could it be the whole set of bloody events came down to a dispute between two fragmented social movements over the possession of *As You Like It*?"

Coming to this conclusion, Marx relaxed and felt some temptation as he fingered a cheroot in his inner pocket. No, he said to himself, a second one today might bring on further congestion. What, then?

Walking along past a string of cafés, he noticed all the sunny, sparkling faces of the edifices, caressed by the wheel of the sun. He could imagine his own penetration throwing radiance on the dark spaces of these crimes. Then, something else captured his attention.

Lunch was near. He was under a strict dietary rule, laid down by the imperious Feckles, yes, but even so, passing the Parisian Café and glancing at an outdoor table where Mrs. Smallweed was sitting, he fell in love with a sparkling ginger ice she was consuming and pulled up a chair by her side to have one.

Chapter 15

As soon as Eleanor entered the Pembroke apartments, she heard the news: Captain Von Pelt had been killed by a ghost. She fainted.

The details were that Mary Van Winkle had gone riding into the country accompanied by Von Pelt. They reached a bridge over a mountain pass. A rifle spoke. He plunged from his horse.

It was known that the late Van Winkle was a crack shot, so—and how could one think otherwise, given the millionaire's jealousy—everyone said old Van Winkle had acted from beyond the grave.

Held up and fanned by three gentlemen, Eleanor was gently deposited on a settee while Swandra took up the fanning. Coming out of her daze, Tussy told the maid to stop pestering her with air in her face and then, after straightening her jerkin, asked Swandra to sit down beside her.

"My lady," Swandra said, "that's against protocol."

"Oh, pooh. Sit right here." Eleanor patted the seat. "You can go back to fanning, but not so strenuously."

"I have other duties," the maid protested.

"Just explain this new thing, this new tragedy, and then you can go." She knew Swandra couldn't resist gossiping.

Another move, after sitting, Swandra leaned closer so that Eleanor could see the sweat on her forehead, drawing a line along her tied-back russet hair.

"There is a bridge," the woman told her. "I know it well. It's called the Lovers' Catapult."

"Name comes from a legend, I venture," Eleanor said.

"The story goes that a pair of star-crossed sweethearts, forbidden by their family to marry, came to the bridge planning suicide. He was an adjutant and, on that fateful evening, the only transport he could obtain was a wagon pulling a siege catapult. On an inspiration of the moment, they seated themselves on the infernal machine, lit torches, and launched off into space."

"Keep fanning."

"Another legend," Swandra continued. "They say that whenever a terrible crime is about to be perpetrated—I mean in the vicinity of the crossing—suddenly ghost torches will come flying through the air to scare off the culprit."

"But legends aside," Eleanor prodded.

"But there are so many attached to that spot."

"Yes?" Eleanor asked, willing to go on.

"There's the Wolf-Head Parade, which will be commemorated tonight."

"Pray tell."

Swandra elaborated, "The noble Prince Stanislaw had been out hunting in the forest and, as the sun went down, he became separated from his band and was trapped and surrounded by brigands. He was saved by the sudden descent of wolves, which came swarming down from the cliffs and savaged their way through the robbers, leaving the prince unscathed. To memorialize this miraculous event, men dressed in wolf heads picked up torches and marched through the town. The torches were those of Stanislaw's band, who followed the wolves' growls to locate their lost master."

Eleanor brought her back to Von Pelt. "But today's event is not a legend. Please tell me exactly what happened."

It would have been impossible for Swandra to report such things as the conversations of the riders, whom Eleanor had seen ride past her this morning, but later, when

Eleanor knew more of what was going on, she felt she could visualize how the murder had taken place.

~

The road in the mountains rose quickly through the trees till it began wending along a ridge that took them through a craggy area. As if they were framed in foliage, the mammoth, rugged gray cliffs had woods below in the forest and firs steepling their tops.

Mary noticed the captain was riding the same roan mare he had shown off in the meadow and had the same undecorated, commonplace bridle and saddle.

They rode companionably side by side as Mary talked. "Of course, I hunger to get back to the gaming tables. My husband brought plenty of money, but somehow it's tied up in a special account he was using to buy the Shakespeare folio from that woman. Aha."

Von Pelt couldn't believe they were spending so much money on a book. Was Shakespeare that valuable?

"I think," Mary explained, "part of the reason Henry got it in his bonnet to get the book is that there is a romantic tale attached to it."

She told him again how she loved these poetic Eastern European intrigues and adventures. "Shortly after we arrived at the spa, Frau Feckles approached my husband with an offer of the book, and she gave him its history.

"Two days after Kugelmann had killed his paramour, Frau Feckles found the book while cleaning her husband's library. She guessed the assassin had put it there for safekeeping after obtaining it from some collection. Ultimately, she surmised it would have been used to support the Serbian cause. She hid it."

"She didn't think of turning it over to her husband?" Von Pelt asked.

"She had a bad marriage, and this was her ticket out.

Since she kept it from her spouse, my husband could only visit her to negotiate at night when her husband was out of town."

"A devious one, this Frau."

Mary went on, "After finding it, she hid it at her sister's, which was prescient, since when she and her husband went on vacation, their house was ransacked. The Serbs must have been on the scent."

Von Pelt reined up his roan and pointed to a large falcon swooping past them toward the cliffs. It was white-orange, mottled with black markings that resembled leaves. As it turned, Mary could see that on the wings, the black accents had enlarged, so only a trace of orange shone through.

Von Pelt clicked his tongue. "I've always dreamed of owning one of those magnificent warriors."

"Have you been listening?" she queried.

"Every word."

"While I was prison, I was thinking that maybe these Serbians were behind my husband's murder."

The road fell back into thicker forest, making their ride cooler if less picturesque.

Von Pelt, who had pulled ahead, now dropped back. "I can't work that out."

Mary replied, "I think they learned Frau Feckles had the folio and was selling it to my husband. That means she must have it on the premises. They killed my husband to forestall the sale—believe me, these fanatics happily wade through blood to achieve their ends—and in a couple of days they will kill the Feckleses and take the book."

Von Pelt put another question to her. "You said your husband was close-mouthed, so how would the Serbs know about his buying the book?"

"That's the puzzle piece I put in place in the jail. Molly had no love for me. She must have overheard us talk about the book and passed it on to her playmate Swandra, whom she met in Versailles. The woman's a Serb fire-eater. That set the crime afoot."

"And they kill Molly as a reward for the information," Von Pelt said skeptically.

The lane took a dip, dropping down to a hollow crossed by a bridge.

Not answering Von Pelt's comment, Mary spurred her horse and galloped down to the center of the bridge, where she knew there was a magnificent vista. Von Pelt was soon at her side, and they looked into the distance at the twin spires of St. Mary Magdalene, visible through a downslope of trees. Karlsbad appeared fragmented, shunting together the woods' green and the circus colors of the town.

The two servants accompanying them hung back to where the bridge began.

Mary luxuriated. A lazy sweep of wind played in her hair, making the top strands spring away from her head. She experienced the pleasant smell of her horse and the touch of sweat on the dimples on her forehead.

She looked with some fondness at Von Pelt. A make-shift confederacy had grown between them because they were both devoted gamblers barred from play. After they'd spoken at the picnic, he'd approached her and talked of his love of the casino. Her husband had seen her having an innocent conversation about their mutual vice and exploded in a jealous fit at Ludwig's.

Mary took her feet from the stirrups, preparing to dismount. She wanted to walk around a little to relax her legs. Von Pelt said, "Do you see that magnificent bird up aloft?"

Before she could follow his pointing arm, there was a loud crack as if a branch had broken, and he toppled from his horse, landing on the bridge's broad parapet.

She couldn't comprehend what was happening. Her horse reared and threw her. She landed heavily on her arm, which filled with pain.

Dazed for a moment, she heard the servants' horses thundering down the incline. They dismounted, and one of them tried to lift her, causing her to scream, and under that she heard Von Pelt crying, "Help me. You've got to help me."

The servant at her side was still meddling with her. "Don't lift me," she squawked. "I've broken my arm."

She winced in pain but eased herself up. "Reinhold, what's going on?"

"The captain was shot."

For a minute she lost the import of that, but she fought back her nausea. The scene started to revolve as if she had boarded a slow carousel, but she bit into the side of her mouth and held her surroundings fast. "How bad is he hurt?"

The other servant, Hans, came up crying and saying, "It shouldn't be. I don't know how to ever, ever—"

Mary was regaining some of her pluck. "Shush up, dear. Just tell me how bad it is. Did they kill him?"

More crying from Hans. "I don't know. I just don't know."

Reinhold had gone to the parapet, and now he came back. "He doesn't know because the good captain has fallen into the gulf."

Hans said, "I was trying to help him up and he convulsed. It was impossible to save him."

When she heard her husband had been murdered, Mary had cried nonstop for an hour, two hours, locked up in jail, whimpering and sobbing. Then she had bit her lip and gone on. How pathetic, she thought. Had she cried so deeply for her first husband and all the Confederate dead?

But the shock of Von Pelt's death was more overpowering in that it had happened while in a way not happening— since she had never seen the wounded body—right in front of her. She tried and failed to close off the rain of tears.

∽

After Swandra told her what had happened, the maid spoke superstitiously. "Begging your pardon, mum, but certain areas are primed for tragedies. One death leads to another, and the Catapult, having already been cursed once, long ago, naturally attracted a new killing to its structure."

"I wouldn't call that very scientific," Eleanor said dryly.

"Haven't you noticed how, after a murder is committed at a certain location, the place has an aura? People will avoid passing it, or they will stare at the site with dark fascination?"

"And they are seeing the leftover aura of the curse?" Eleanor said, unbelieving.

She settled back and closed her eyes. She found all this talk of premonitions annoying, even in Shakespeare. Wasn't it really simply a cloudy remembrance of the type of dirty past with which in *Richard III* Old Queen Margaret, who sees this past more clearly, torments Queen Elizabeth after her downfall?

> Thus hast the court of justice wheel'd about,
> And left thee but a very prey of time;
> Having no more thought of what thou wast,
> To torture thee the more, being what thou art.

To Eleanor, all this talk of emanations and miasmas was but a ciphered way to express the brass weight of history.

Swandra stood up and was stepping away as, Eleanor now perceived, Lady Pembroke approached at the gallop.

The good lady had a chalky face, her wrinkles powdered under. Her stringy hair seemed to have been whitened by this same powder. Eleanor knew she always wore a happy expression, put on her face by an act of will, not the product of a gaiety bubbling up from an inner spring, as one saw, for example, in her sister Laura.

Pembroke wore a lovely, pink, two-piece ensemble with a very prominent back bustle. In front, the skirt was so arranged that one layer was peeled back and pinned to the next, so it looked like a curtain drawn aside for a peep outdoors.

The good lady snapped to Swandra, "Does she still need attention? You have other duties, you know."

Swandra was already on her feet. "Apologies, my lady."

Eleanor got up to stand beside her. "I'm sorry I detained her so long. My fault, all."

With that, Pembroke nodded her head sympathetically while Swandra scooted off. After chatting a moment with their host, Eleanor crossed the crowded room and discreetly let herself out of the miasma.

Chapter 16

Being a professional detective often demands one be cagey and able to adroitly manipulate others, especially one's parents.

After learning Yvette had stayed in the maid's quarters, sick, Sherlock approached his father, first mentioning that Yvette, who had helped in their rooms, was ill. Father, who was preparing for lunch—and once he finished eating would begin preparing for dinner—frowned. His frown was not one of displeasure, but of having to do the mental work of recalling the woman's face and form, as he had so many people to recognize on this rare trip away from his house. As he had told his son, he preferred life at the homestead, where there was the same round of fellow gentry, trades-people, and tenants, year in and year out, none with foreign names, all as stable and unchanging as good British beef.

Sherlock gave him a leg up. "Yvette is the maid who came in right after Mama lost her brooch. Gee, she was on the point of accusing the girl of filching it when I reminded her it was a different girl who had come the previous day when she'd first missed it."

"Bad show, that."

"And then, you'll remember, Yvette found the brooch when she was sweeping up."

"Clever girl," Father said, checking his pockets for his tobacco pouch.

"Your tobacco is on the sideboard," Sherlock noted.

"Oh, yes, so it is."

His father had his wrapped bowtie unfastened, hanging

loose. He wore it over a checked vest and counterchecked pants. His face was decorated with muttonchops, whiskers forming a stripe that ran under but not in front of his chin in a kind of trellis. He was usually red-faced, not from choler but overheating. His look could be indulgent or censorious, eyes and mouth modified accordingly.

"So, she calmed the old girl's fears. It's the traveling that gets to them," Father commented, referring to women.

"And I kept thinking," Sherlock went on, finishing a thought, "that we, you and I together ..." He seemed to be losing his usual precision of speech. "A token, now that, being sick ..."

Apparently, Sherlock's father, Lionel, previously distracted in looking for his pipe and tobacco, now listened more closely and deciphered more unerringly his son's slightly cracked diction than he had the boy's straightforward statements. "Sixteen, quite the man, already an eye for the ladies. Bit of fine fluff, that Yvette."

Just then Fidge came wandering through. She loved frills and had adorned her maid's uniform with a wool flower sewn on the side of her hat. On the shoulder straps of her white oversmock were placed a couple of embroidered roses. Sherlock thought of her as a walking hatchet, both in her face and in the way she spoke, cutting off words and phrases with a sharp intonation of breath.

Lionel hustled her out. "What is this, a railroad platform? The son and I are having a little unchesting, man to man. Be gone."

"You mistake me, Father," Sherlock said as Fidge doddered out.

"Maybe so, maybe so," Lionel answered as his hands again rustled through his vest to emerge with a change purse. He plucked out four small silver coins, then fisted them and held them above Sherlock's hands. The boy quickly caught his drift and cupped his hands below so the coins could trickle down into them as if they were acorns shaken from a tree. Brightly, Father said, "With our good wishes that she get better," before going back to tut-tutting and filling his pipe, which first had to be located, as it had wandered off.

Sherlock left the apartments graciously enough, although cursing himself for having to go through this (in his eyes) humiliating experience because he had spent not only his allowance but a small nest egg he had been nursing on a very small necklace.

Yvette lived on the less-tenanted south side of the river. His plan was to drop in on her, perhaps get to know her better, and then go to Wong's to find out about the laundry girl. He wanted to know why she had attended the late meeting of the Communards.

After crossing the bridge, Sherlock walked from the sanitarium precincts of the city into the alleys and small lanes where the maids and other workers resided, and it seemed as if he were going from the finely lacquered to the unvarnished. The pristine streets along the Teplá featured cleaned, pastel building facades, looking like well-scrubbed faces, fronting spotless sidewalks, which were festooned with freestanding trees and tidy little bushes in basins. Many shops had hanging plants strung up around their doors.

This was Sherlock's first time venturing out of the city's centers to stray into the outlying districts, which ran right up to the mountains' tailings. The pavement gave way to dirt tracks. Here one left the artificially forested quadrants of the spas and entered areas darkened by the mountains' shade. The streets weren't as policed for litter, and one could see occasional boxes and other trash lying about. Even the building fronts, half-lit, were of different complexion. Instead of sprightly shops and well-looked-after residences, the edifices were either workshops or dorms with drab, grayed-out faces. As Sherlock threaded deeper into the territory, moving through lattices of shadow, he felt as if he were a Dupin-like detective penetrating into Montmartre.

Sherlock turned into the maid's apartment complex, where he met the doorman, a chubby little cherub of a fellow who, like his Christmas version, was hanging on a tree. To put that more precisely, he was on a ladder, half on it, pruning a large bush, which had the appearance of a magnified feather duster, and was leaning so far into the plant he had almost become an ornament. It was his doorkeeper's jacket, not his present task, that alerted Sherlock as to his occupation. The boy went up to him, steadied the ladder, and said he'd come to see about Mademoiselle Yvette.

That must have been a surprising or unsettling question, judging by the tremors it stirred up in the bush. Delicately turning himself around, using a handful of branches for balance, the short fellow who, from his perch, towered over Holmes said, "We don't take male visitors here."

"Yes, I suspected as much," Holmes returned, visoring his eyes with a palm as he looked upward into the sun. "I thought I might ask her to come down to the parlor if she is feeling any better."

The doorkeeper descended the ladder and, turning around, shading his eyes, looked up at the building's windows as if he couldn't talk about Yvette without facing her. "I can't rightly do that," he said. Then, dropping his sunshade but keeping his head cocked at the same angle to peer at the six-foot-tall youth, he added, "A guest, then?"

"Yes," the youth said, offering his hand. "I'm Sherlock Holmes."

Not seeming to know what a handshake was, the man ignored the proffer and said, reluctantly, "I'm Herr Glatt," and then added, even more reluctantly, "at your service."

Perhaps, Sherlock thought, *the man is thinking of a better employment of his hands*, and with that the young man drew out one of the coins his father had forked out to him. "It doesn't seem as if it would be much trouble," he said, using his right hand to wipe off perspiration from his brow while his left, as if all unaware of what the other hand was doing, held out the silver.

It couldn't have been snapped up any faster if it were a breadcrumb dropped into a teeming fishbowl.

"Could you take her my message?" Holmes asked, now with a reasonable hope of compliance.

"She's out."

"I thought she was sick?"

"Miraculous quick recovery," Glatt said, then struck a pose, head on chin, staring back into the bush.

Sherlock was not sure how to take this and asked, "Is there some problem?"

"I'm just thinking."

"Oh."

"She went off with a friend to a picnic, but I can't quite remember where." His hands, too, had separate minds, for one, the right, clasped his chin as an aid to thought and the other, the left, rubbed its fingers in the palm in the universal gesture signifying "money."

Sherlock added a second coin to supplement his first and to help provoke further memories.

Glatt recalled, "Take the second road north out from the end of Vítězná Drahomířino, then follow the highway up till you take the second trail that branches off near the three-kilometer road marker, a bright red one. Go down that path a short distance and you'll find a pleasant meadow, bedecked with flowers and two young maidens."

"She informed you of all this?"

"I have to know where she is in case of emergencies. Things come up."

Conversation ended, Glatt remounted the rickety ladder, and Sherlock set off trailblazing. True to Glatt's words, once

Sherlock had worked his way out of town, he found near the red mile marker a trail going left. As he reached the turnoff, he was overtaken by a hotel guest, one Stratford, a nodding acquaintance, who was rushing up the road, he explained, to find his wife, who was at the archery range. He wanted to tell her the shocking news of Von Pelt's murder. Exciting as this was, it also became another excuse Sherlock could use to approach the picnickers.

Off the highway, the woods were quite thick, many of the trees flowering with white blossoms on their branches, as if they were lathered up and emerging from a bath. The ground around them was weeded with shadows, making the area too dark and overhung to see very far. After a short walk, he came to a clearing where the grass was pillowed and freckled with blue flowers. In the center, maids Yvette and Swandra had spread out a hotel tablecloth in a sprig of flat space, and the two leaned close, talking seriously, sitting beside a bottle of wine and a spread of bread and cheese.

Swandra had been saying something but immediately silenced herself when Sherlock was seen on the way. All he got was: "If General Trochu had actually taken measures to—"

His advent caused a stir; Yvette jumped up, and Swandra stayed just sitting but was smoothing her blue skirt and brushing away crumbs.

Sherlock took in Swandra at a glance. Out of uniform, she wore a red bodice with pure white sleeves attached, both of which vividly played against the color of the black skirt, which was mostly covered by a white apron. On her head was a straw hat that complemented the ringlets of her russet hair.

"What have we here?" Yvette said, coming toward him.

One glance at her and all the words flew out of his mind. Her brown eyes, sparkling, were sharp-tenored; that is, they cut through everything. She had a sharp nose, thin lips, as if barely penciled in, and a cleft chin, all topped off by cropped brown hair, lustrous as a chestnut bay's. Dressed in a white blouse and floor-length blue dress, as she moved closer what he was struck by most was her insouciance, which was a quality dimmed down, dimmed out almost, as she performed her role as a maid. He had thought of her as quiet, studious, the polar opposite of the brassy Eleanor, so the revelation of this new side of her was as stupendous as if from a dreary wood there emerged a dark, flower-bedecked dryad.

"What brings you to our picnic?" Yvette asked. "I can't believe this is by chance."

Swandra was rustling through their hamper and fished out a third wine glass. "Be prepared," she said, smiling and pouring some white wine.

Sherlock said, "I have some news which I think you would want to hear."

Yvette replied, showing her own form of pique, "The news I want to know is how you found us here."

He was flustered, but pushed on. "I talked to your gate master, Herr Glatt. He thought you'd want to learn this latest turn of events, so he pointed me the way."

"The bastard," Swandra said, having quickly lost her tranquility.

"Two points: give to us quickly your news and be off," Yvette said saucily.

Sherlock had, not even thinking about it, been awaiting the wine, and now Yvette firmly but decisively seized Swandra's wrist as she was in the act of passing it and had her set the third glass beside her folded legs.

They sat back on their haunches, the blond and the brunette, each of their hairdos reflecting the crescents of bright sunlight in different, equally appealing manners.

He said almost ruthlessly, "Von Pelt was shot down and killed at the Lovers' Catapult Bridge."

Swandra was the more emotional, Yvette the more verbal of the pair. The first gasped, sucking in her breath, and the second said distractedly, "Are you satisfied?"

Swandra began sobbing. Yvette, who had lifted herself to her full height, though not standing up but staying on her knees, now sank back lower so she could throw her arms around Swandra's shoulders. "Come, dear," Yvette said.

If by Sherlock's inspiration in bringing up the news of Von Pelt's death, he had hoped to create a revealing commotion that would help unravel the case, he had succeeded only in part. There was plenty of commotion, but what was going on was darker than ever.

"Okay," Yvette said, "we have your news and there is no more need of you." She punctuated her angry words by drinking off the third glass of wine, not losing hold of Swandra's shoulders. "We wanted some free time, just a little, because we're facing a long evening's work at the Hunter's Ball tonight. Not only do we have to hand around food tidbits, but we must dress up as sheep."

"Sheep?"

"All the maids wear sheep ears, and the manservants wear those of wolves. That idiot Bosch came up with the idea. I hope they don't make us pour drinks."

Suiting actions to the opposite of words, Yvette poured two more glasses, tossing one off and offering the other to head-buried Swandra, who refused it. Again, looking around as if she had been drowsy and just woken up and spotted Sherlock for the first time, she handed him over the glass.

"I didn't know Swandra would be so affected by the news of this death," he said, "I apologize for intruding." He realized the best apology would be to exit.

"We'd have to learn about it sooner or later," Yvette said.

Another thunder of tears from her partner.

Sherlock steeled himself, gulped down the wine, and

stood. He was overruling all his inclinations, except common sense, in leaving. He had meant to learn about the Commune group and had gotten nothing. He'd also wanted to establish a possibly friendly footing with Yvette. Instead, he so upset her that she might never talk to him again.

Heavy weights to carry as he trudged, footsore and saddened, back toward Karlsbad. He could have been a fleeing Communard, sneaking through a field while behind him in the distance shone the shattered red flames of the burning City of Light.

Chapter 17

The day kept getting hotter and hotter, so Eleanor suggested that after a late lunch the three of them—Sherlock, her father, and herself—retire to the darkness and coolness of the Karlsbad lending library.

～

Browsing the shelves, Marx was surprised to find a copy of Hegel's *Logic*. For years he had toyed with rereading it. However, as he opened the book he did so mechanically, worrying anew, after he'd thought this fear was becalmed, that Sherlock might find a way to make trouble if he had indeed learned Marx's true identity.

On the surface and below the surface too, it was an absurd thought. Eleanor and he were leaving Bohemia in a few days, and Hubner, a fair representative of the authorities' attitude, had shown he was unconcerned with Marx's political background. This Sherlock apprehension was the type of nagging worry that would come up when he was trying to sleep. Tossing and turning, Marx would be swept by thoughts of the string of disasters that had plagued radical republicans and good socialists with the fall of the Commune. He would think of his unfinished work, of books he needed to consult, and of Eleanor's cracked love affair. For the last few nights, Sherlock had joined the list of insomniac annoyances.

He read a passage in the Hegel: "Dialectic's purpose is to study things in their own being and movement and thus to demonstrate the finitude of the partial categories of the understanding." He savored the reading as if it were a homily that he could apply to his troubles.

To forget this worry, Hegel seemed to be telling him, he couldn't isolate it as a partial category, but had to see it as part of the topsy-turvy whole. He should consider Sherlock not as an individual annoyance, but as making up part of the large kaleidoscope of Britain, Bohemia, and Paris. Marx told himself that he had, like a dummkopf, simply displaced all his multiform anxieties onto this innocent boy.

He glanced over at Sherlock, who was flipping over the pages of a newspaper.

~

Sherlock, after visiting with Yvette and later Herr Wong, had come to a guesswork conclusion as to who had shot Von Pelt. As a lark, he'd decided to try out Dupin's method of searching for clues in the newspaper to confirm his tentative inference.

The paper's most implausible rumor, in reporting the new murder, was that Mary Van Winkle had started an affair with Von Pelt before her husband's demise. Envenomed against her spouse by her being made the object of sport in this public display at Ludwig's, she had killed him and Molly, a witness of her crime. Somehow she had escaped justice and, being as brazen as your typical American, within twenty-four hours of her release from prison, she went off for a forest ride with her paramour, *apparently* to visit the Freudenbergs, but *transparently* to visit an inn along the way for illicit afternoon delight. Justice couldn't stop her, concern for public outrage did not dissuade her, and of morals, she had none. It was in such a situation, one that cried out to the heavens for justice, that the old Van Winkle's ghost came back to earth and killed the usurper of his wife's affection.

Die Zeit offered an interesting tidbit, which could be woven into other information. It said, "Von Pelt was seldom if ever seen on this highway. As we hear, he would only make short excursions down our area's beautiful mountain trails, taking his riding students on short jaunts, hugging the edge of the city. Some have voiced the idea that he was tied to the town by the apron strings of a pretty little maid."

The sniper would need to have planned this killing in advance. Since Von Pelt never took this road on his excursions, the trap could not have been set for him. So, presumably, the shot had taken down the wrong target.

Sherlock withdrew his notebook, another key element in the junior detective's toolkit. In it he had noted down a line that had appeared in the paper on the day of the murder: "Kugelman, the assassin who escaped two weeks ago, was seen last week in the Black Forest on the road toward Darmsbach. He had set up a blind above the Lovers' Catapult Bridge but was flushed from there and is about to be apprehended." So, disregarding the falsehood in the paper's statement that this blind had been fashioned by Kugelmann, it could be surmised that the killing of Mary Van Winkle had long been premeditated.

There was one telling detail about the blind in *Der Tagesspiegel*: "Around the site where the bloodthirsty assassin had crouched for hours above the Catapult Bridge were crumbs of bread and cheese and also strange ashy flakes one officer said reminded him of the remains of burnt opium."

He had learned Mary had stood in the gauntlet line, attacking and reviling the captured Communards. He could imagine the toyshop group of ex-Parisians had little love for her. Among the exiles was Miss Chung, who might have been puffing opium as she waited in her blind.

However, the most convincing evidence in this respect came in his earlier talk with Herr Wong. Wong stated that Chung had been in Paris when it fell to the right-wing French army. She had gotten here in a company led by François. Moreover, Sherlock learned, she was not happy in Karlsbad, where there were only a couple of Asians. She yearned to return to Paris, where the once-substantial Chinese community had reformed.

Contemplating these facts and what he had inferred from the newspapers, Sherlock said to himself, "Now you have your ghost."

His next intellectual endeavor was less successful. He tried to imagine himself into the mind of the murderer. He abruptly realized he was relying on ideas he had gotten from dime novel stereotypes. These were the product of perfervid imaginations, not the study of hard facts.

These penny dreadfuls were filled with caricatures, something brought home to him by his acquaintance with Marx and his daughter. People like them, Communist agitators, appeared in the pulps as rabble-rousing charlatans with no real interest in the cause but only in getting fame and pelf. He had brought this up, obliquely, with Eleanor, who had told him the same appeared in books by higher-class authors such as Eliot's *Felix Holt* and Charlotte Bronte's *Shirley*. It was a literary tradition going all the way back to *Henry VI, Part 2*, in which Jake Cade leads a crowd of tinkers and village craftsman in what he calls a fight for plebian democracy, but which is really a naked grab for power in which Cade hopes to make himself chief.

These caricatures, as well as those in Oily or Sergeant Cuff, didn't resemble the real thing. The stereotypical rebel leaders hardly had the serious-minded outlook and worked-out methodology of Marx. The man had once advised him to work slowly, digging through all the hard facts but then putting them into wider patterns. As a guide, he told Sherlock to look into Hegel.

Sherlock was more likely to stride blindfolded into London traffic than to sit down with a head-scratching read like Hegel, but he did pretend to acquiesce.

"First read Hegel's *Elementary Logic*," Marx told him.

"Yes," Sherlock said, "*Elementary*. I've got it. *Elementary*."

The bomb-loaded revolutionaries in the penny dread-fuls also didn't have charming daughters like Eleanor who were an oddly attractive combination of fearlessness and timidity. And she listened, really listened, to him in a way other grown-ups never did.

So, try as he might, Sherlock couldn't quite visualize how Miss Chung had acted as an assassin, though he was convinced she had been.

~

Yi-Yi Chung rode her borrowed horse down the mountain till she reached a branch-off that led to the cliff's summit.

She wore a black, tunic-like top with wide sleeves, loose-fitting black trousers, and black slippers.

She was of medium height and thin with the dark skin of Southeast Asia. She had semicircle tattoos beneath her eyebrows to make her brown eyes look larger, as well as a broad nose and perpetually smiling mouth. Her braids were divided in two and tied on the top of her head so they stuck up like animal ears. They resembled those of the *wu li jing*, the fox who changed into a beautiful woman to entrap and punish evil men.

When she reached the ascending path, she tied the animal, unpacked her rifle and supplies, and climbed up to where her fellow ex-Communards had set up a concealed sniper post, the one the police had found and broken up.

She didn't need such an elaborate setup. Near the edge, they had cut a knothole in the bushes through which she could see the bridge. She needed no rest to hold the rifle steady.

The sun was just lugging its bulk past the cliffs that faced off on the other side of the road, sprinkling first gleams of light like sudden flashes of tinsel in the trees. In a few minutes, an ocean of light swelled out to illuminate the lovely vistas of cliff, forest, and blue space, constantly deepening in brilliance and increasing in heat.

She had heard there were places like this in China, but she had never been to China.

When she arrived in Karlsbad, pushed in her flight from the overthrown Commune and pulled by François, who led a little band of refugees, she was taken in by Wong. He was foreman of the laundry establishment attached to the Hotel Pupp. It was Wong who gave her a book, called 头腦控制的贵族, on calming oneself through breathing exercises.

She sat on a broken log in the cleared space and placed her forearms on her raised knees, palms up. She closed her eyes, took three breaths, and meditated. The mandarins advised you to let your mind move systematically along the chakras, first in the center of the forehead, then on the top of the head, then at the back of neck, and then down the spine and back up again. But she tended to lose sight of this progress and think back on her life.

She had been born in the French colony of Cochin-China on a farm on the outskirts of Gia Đinh to Chinese immigrants. The landlord pressed them too hard, so the children had to be sold. At fourteen, she was taken to the port; money changed hands, and a few months later she was in a brothel in Marseilles.

After three years there, she contacted tuberculosis, and the madam allowed her brother, who was a sailor on foreign ships, to take her out. They went to Paris, where the small Chinese community welcomed them and where they found laundry work.

She healed slowly, imperfectly, in a few years, and then the Prussians surrounded the city. Things became both better and worse. Yi-Yi and her brother knew how to starve and helped the others, the Westerners, to endure.

It was at this point that hearts opened everywhere, and the standoffish French embraced them. It was as if a jewel box had sat locked on a shelf all these years and was now opened and disgorging its hidden riches. She joined a woman's militia, worked in the communal garden, and was a leader of the block committee. The mysterious world of Europe grew visible.

As she knew, such moments of fierce tranquility are always short-lived. The reactionary army broke in; her brother was killed in the fighting, and she and a few others sought haven in Karlsbad, where Yi-Yi remet Swandra.

Swandra had been a maid using their laundry in Paris until her master's family moved to Versailles. They shared many memories and decided to become sworn sisters (结拜姐妹). With Wong's help, they went to a glade in the forest and set up a small altar, placing on it fruit and flowers. Each lit incense and pledged, "By the Jade Emperor above and King Yama below, I take an oath to support and protect my sister."

Before they began, Yi-Yi had asked Wong, "Don't we need a Taoist to be present to make it official?"

Wong nodded upward. "The moon will be your witness."

With Swandra, Yi-Yi attended meetings with the other exiles called to raise funds and discuss impractical schemes of retaliation. Then Mary Van Winkle arrived in town. Swandra had told them how Mary had led a contingent of Americans to the gauntlet where Communard prisoners were hooted at and pelted with stones. Swandra again ranted against Mary, but when the woman stole her boyfriend, she asked if anyone would dare to kill her.

At first Yi-Yi did not respond, but she knew as a sworn sister, her responsibility was heavy, so she volunteered to act as villainess, planning to return to Paris if she managed to escape. However, something new made the group reconsider this attendant. They learned from Molly about the folio, which some members said they could seize and sell for funding. Ironically, Molly regretted passing along the information, for she became the one voice in their little conclave advising, since we had a woman willing to take up the task, that we just kill Mary outright. But now, with her husband dead and Mary likely to leave any minute while the book was who knows where, every compunction was set aside and her fellows got Yi-Yi a horse and rifle.

After finishing her meditation and eating the bread and cheese she had packed, Yi-Yi lit a stick of incense and offered a prayer to the god of war. Then she sat back to wait.

Two hours later, she heard movement on the road. Mary and the Prussian captain came riding onto the bridge. Even as Yi-Yi tracked them with her sight, worrying about taking down a moving target, they halted their horses right below her on the overpass.

Yi-Yi was coated with a second layer of sweat beyond the one produced by the thick undergrowth. She only had one cartridge.

She had lied to François and the others. She had never used a rifle. She had trained over and over with the women's militia but had not been in the thick of battle.

Yi-Yi steadied herself. Mary with her mannish outfit might have been a Chinese woman. Von Pelt with his stiff, awkward movements might have been a mandarin.

Yi-Yi shot and missed the quarry.

～

Eleanor glanced over and saw Sherlock looking toward her, but blankly, as if he were seeing only inside his head.

She went back to the Bard. She was not seeking clues—how could she be?—but inspiration on how to proceed, just as how in olden time, Puritans would consult Bibles as if they were books of spells. The fanatics would pose a question, then open the good book at random; the verse the seeker alighted upon was taken as an answer.

Eleanor, less superstitiously, was trying to "flashpoint

her thoughts." By that phrase, she connoted an experience she occasionally had when reading. At the very tindered, far edges of consciousness, an idea would pass like a chimeric beast half seen in the twilight woods, one markedly different from her usual thought train. If she managed to seize that flash, she would find herself looking from a new, swiveled perspective. Something like that happened now as she skimmed *As You Like It*. Her sensation was similar to her infrequent experience of déjà vu, when something she was going through in reality resembled a scenario or a spoken sentence she had previously assembled in a dream.

It had to be admitted that the plot of *As You Like It* bore some resemblance to their present situation. Shakespeare opens with a double exile, both that of Orlando, sibling of a tyrannical elder brother, and that of Rosalind, daughter of the already banished Duke Senior. Both leave the court of Duke Frederick to hide in the forest of Arden. So, everyone has moved into a liminal space. Circumstantially different, since everyone was in Karlsbad by choice, but, even so, Eleanor and her father had left their usual stamping grounds in London and come on vacation to this forested glen.

Again, there is no murder in Shakespeare, but there is, as in Karlsbad, slippage from identity to identity. Rosalind, who leaves the court with her friend Celia, disguises herself as a man so they can travel more securely. Before everyone was packed off from court, Rosalind had met and been smitten with Orlando, and he with her. Now, turnabout, Orlando, meeting her in the woods and accepting her disguise as the male Ganymede, confesses his love for the seemingly distant Rosalind. The undercover Ganymede proposes a fetching game. To give him practice and relief, Ganymede will act as a stand-in for Rosalind, allowing Orlando to profess love to him (her) as a way to vent his tortured feelings.

In Karlsbad, too, there was a game of disguise and false

face. Swandra and Heidi on the surface were nothing but faithful spa attendants, while off this stage they acted to upend the whole of Austria-Hungary and aided criminals who dealt in purloined folios.

Eleanor dipped in the play and found what she was looking for: a passage that caused a set of flashpoints to skim through her awareness. The passage that awakened her occurred when Orlando first entered the woods of his exile, thinking he had left Rosalind behind forever. He decides to memorialize his feelings by pasting her name on trees and hanging love poems on their branches: "Hang there my verse, in witness of my love." He apostrophizes her: "O Rosalind, these trees shall be my books, // And in their barks my thoughts I'll character // That every eye which in this forest looks // Shall see thy virtue witnessed everywhere." The poems he hangs up themselves do the talking: "Tongues I'll hang on every tree."

The embered thought, forming a momentary, melting brocade in her mind's underreaches, was this: *The ticket that Sherlock found on the roof, sticking out of the gutter, that was the key, standing ready if I but turn it.*

Hadn't every penny dreadful mystery she'd read, including those of Helen Trueblood, shown a villain exposed by the detective's feigned knowledge?

It was not that this person, hiding on the roof, had committed or instigated any of the murders. The point was that there must have been some activity going on to peep at. If, she reasoned, Peeping Toms or Thomasinas do not like to be exposed, then the ploy she was mulling would make the individual realize his or her name would be made public if he or she didn't confess to them about the nocturnal snooping.

Closing the book, she sketched out the plan, which entailed taking Sherlock to the Hunter's Ball, where they would go to dance, waltzing and sleuthing the night away.

Chapter 18

Eleanor came up with the plan, bought the tickets, and obtained a feline costume. She and Sherlock talked to Sergeant Hubner about their scheme, and he agreed to participate.

Hubner would make an announcement at the ball—if the spy had had a ball ticket on the roof, he must be planning to attend—that would say the police had found a partial ticket stub that had fluttered down from the pump room roof, and tomorrow the police would go to the roof to find the missing half, which, due to the numbers on the first half of the stub, would reveal who had been up there on the night before the crime.

Using a passkey supplied by Heidi via Cranky, Eleanor and Sherlock planned to go into the pump room and conceal themselves behind the water fountains. If, as they hoped would happen, someone came sneaking into the edifice and began ascending the back ladder to reach the roof, then one of them would run to the police while the other maintained watch. They had asked Hubner to have a policeman patrolling the street a block over.

To Eleanor the plan was settled, but Sherlock insisted on a beforehand conference, so they set up a meeting in their hotel's lobby.

Before coming downstairs, Eleanor made a final check of her cat ears in the mirror. She had chosen her best dress, a worn blue one in ray chiffon with lovely folded pleats and a neatly trimmed bustle. She walked into the hall, then, almost as an afterthought, turned back and reentered the room. She went to her desk and tore the temporary letter in half. Now only the letter breaking her engagement with Lissagaray remained.

She went downstairs and found her way to a seat toward the back of the lobby. It was as if she had taken a place in an aviary, as so many peacock feathers surrounded her, standing in elephant-foot stands and grouped together so as to build a hedge around her seat.

Sherlock, carrying a small box, found her there. He wore a Robin Hood costume: brown tunic belted in the center with a square gold buckle, green undersuit and pants, plus black boots with brown cuffs. His pointed round cap would have looked well on an elf. As an accoutrement, he had a hunter's horn slung around his neck.

"What are you bringing?" Eleanor asked as he sat down.

"I got you something, a trinket," the youth replied.

"Why would you do that?" she asked, flattered and confused.

"We've had such interesting dinners and discussions these last weeks, and I've been allowed to contribute even though my opinions often seem unsophisticated. Jove have it, though, I could see that when I made a comment, your father and Cranky were exchanging looks that meant they saw me as a dummkopf or worse. But not you, Eleanor. You take me seriously and never laugh at me."

"That's really not true, dear boy. No one is laughing. Smiling perhaps," Eleanor said. She looked closely to see if he was upset. "Of course, you are young and sometimes haven't read up on what you are talking about, but—"

He broke her off. "It's not that I don't know things. I don't see things."

Eleanor said, "I would say the opposite is the case. You seem to be everywhere, watching everyone. An Argus married to a fleet-footed Mercury." She laughed, not at him but at the awkward situation.

He explained, "When I say I don't see things, I'm think-ing of when you said I look too narrowly. You told me it's only when you see the whole that the parts fit in."

"I would agree to that, though I can't remember ever saying it," Eleanor conceded. "How did I express it? Remind me."

But he shifted and talked of the more recent past. "I went to see Yvette."

"What happened?"

Sherlock said, "I expected to have a quiet tête-à-tête where I might throw in some probing questions."

"Did you learn anything?" Eleanor asked. Judging from his expression, she imagined that, like herself, any tête-à-tête with the opposite sex could lead to disaster.

"She ended up hating me and laughing at me."

"It couldn't have been that bad," Eleanor consoled.

"The smaller situation was blinding me to the larger one."

Eleanor nodded. "That will happen. But I don't know the context here."

"Once in a while, something really big happens, like the Commune, and then for years after, everything that occurs is a repercussion. The murders are repercussions. How each person—Mary, Swandra, Yvette—acts comes out of the impetus of that event. I should have thought about that.

"Hubner told me," the young man went on, "it's as if each person has two selves: the one acting in everyday life, going through the motions, the other driven by the fading thunder of the repercussions, the real motor. He didn't put it exactly like that."

Not knowing precisely how to take this, and worrying about the time, Eleanor sat back in her chair. "So ... what did you get me?"

"Oh, that," Sherlock said. He fumbled with the box, which was wrapped in blue paper. "I wanted to thank you for your kindness in smiling but not laughing at me."

"Hardly reason."

He accidentally tore the paper in handing it over. She opened it to find a small silver design on a necklace chain. "It's so lovely," she said, "although I don't get the symbolism."

"Herr Wong designed it," he said. "You told me you were once called Empress."

"Well."

"This is the Chinese word for cat, to match your ears."

She looked with widened feline eyes at the piece: 貓.

"I'll explain it," Sherlock said. "The left-hand character"—here, he pointed to 豸 —"represents animal, any animal. The lower right-hand box in cat" —he pointed to 田—"means field. The upper right-hand sign indicates young grass." With this, he pointed to the last remaining element, ⁺⁺. "So, the meaning is 'an animal that likes to hide in young grass.'"

"Yes, that's me," Eleanor said with a big smile as she bent down her neck. "Help me fasten it."

Chapter 19

With her beautiful cat-name necklace, Eleanor walked along with Sherlock to the ball. When they arrived at the dance floor, it was already flowing with couples moving to the sprightly polka supplied by an orchestra on a raised dais. Everywhere "animals" were chatting and drinking with hunters at the white-linened tables.

Tables where people might sit and drink were set on a series of small, tiered risers, backed to two walls. The entrance at the far end was like a gate to heaven with its large, gold-spangled and bright white trimming. It led to the vast, polished dance floor that occupied much of the space. The whole room was a study in alabaster. The high-rising walls were as plain as snow sheets except for a series of small pictures set so high they were best viewed by telescope. Picked out among them were scepter lights, which threw gleams into the large pool of illumination created by the shimmering chandeliers, themselves festooned with glass droplets that splayed the light in all directions.

Standing at the entrance, Eleanor glanced deeper into the dancing throng and picked out a female tiger holding a lion tamer close and then a pigeon-headed lady clasped to the breast of an honest woodsman.

They found a table and ordered a white wine. The song had broken off, and new people were moving on and off the floor. A cockatoo sat down at the table next to theirs, her head swaddled in feathers and her partner nowhere in sight. She had one wing in a cast.

"It's Mary Van Winkle," Sherlock said. "What's she doing here?"

Their attention was diverted from staring at the widow to the bandstand. The musicians sat on a platform midway down the hall in a space interrupting the flow of the risers and lifted slightly above them in height. "Ladies and gentlemen," Strauss, the bandmaster, said, "there has been an interesting development in the Van Winkle tragedy, one that concerns everyone here. So, I am going to allow Sergeant Hubner to take the stage for just a moment to acquaint you with it."

Hubner came onstage and said, "Fellow townsmen and visitors, I am appealing to you for help. Tonight, just an hour ago, a ticket to this very ball fluttered to the ground from the roof of the pump room. Presumably, it had been caught in the gutter and some of the repairs that are being done up there dislodged it. Something I can't presume but can only hope is that the possessor of the ticket was hiding on the ceiling at some point when the horrors took place below."

This revelation caused a wave of whispering like the murmuring of leaves when a breeze strikes up.

He continued, "The ticket was torn so that only the last number, five, is there. If we had the full number, we could identify the ticket holder. For now, we are pleading with that person to step forward to help us in our investigation. Tomorrow, my men will give the roof a thorough going over to see if they can find the ticket's other half."

More expressions of excitement came from the crowd, who had gathered in a clump in front of the dais. Now Hubner went off the script they had provided, saying, "May I add that a junior detective who has been instrumental in our search, Sherlock Holmes, with his friend, Eleanor Arbuthnot, found this ticket on the street and have been a great help to our department."

He beamed down on everyone as if he were bestowing prizes for best dancers, not providing information on a criminal case. "So, good friends, let us return to the dance. I will be waiting here for anyone who wants to come forward." As he stepped away, the orchestra launched another waltz.

No one came forward, but Eleanor calculated the mystery man would soon be on the way to the pavilion to retrieve the ticket. It only rested on Sherlock and herself to identify him and report to the policeman stationed nearby.

As they were getting up, Yvette, holding a tray of drinks in one hand and with sheep ears flopping in her hair, passed by. To Sherlock, she threw out, "A-hunting we will go."

"Dash it," Sherlock said. "Eleanor, can you just meet me at the pump room? I'll be along in a half pip. I want to have a final word with Yvette."

Chapter 20

Sherlock scooted out of his seat and followed Yvette, who, even with a tray, moved forward more smoothly than he did. Since he was inexperienced in drinking wine, he was slightly unsteady on his pins from his one glass. His movements were off-center. It was hard to avoid contact, and he nearly unstitched a couple he blundered against. The spinning, disciplined pacings of the tight-waisted men and women whose bustles sheered left and right made him think of the top wall of the planetarium he had visited in London. It was as if, close-up, he were buzzing through the hanging baskets of the gaudy planets, red Marses and ultramarine Venuses.

Once he got through this gauntlet of constellations, he quickly sighted the blue lamb who was moving along the background with an empty tray. He shot off in pursuit with as much excitement as a scavenging wolf who had seen prey, but bending around a woman who was leaving the risers to enter the dance floor, he snagged her skirt with the cord of the hunter's horn around his neck, nearly bringing them both down.

Sherlock unnoosed himself, pouring out excuses, and was back on the scent. He stared here and there, but she had disappeared. Breasting his way past the last table, he went out the entrance to the bar, which was off in a second room. He spied his quarry talking to the barman.

He came up behind. "Yvette."

"So I am," she said, turning and laughing so her flop ears wagged.

"Can I have a brief word?" he begged.

"*Bien sûr, bien sûr. Mais maintenant*, I am hard to work."

He bent in close to offer a whispering retort. "It's about Miss Chung."

The tray rocked, but gently, as if they stood on a ship touched by light waves. She nudged her head left, indicative. "Wait for me back there in the hamper." She was pointing to a door behind the bar. "Jacques," she called to the bartender—who was one of the men he had seen looking at the Paris diorama—and then tossed her head toward Sherlock.

She sailed away, balancing the tray as easily as if it were just another appendage. Sherlock, a trifle dazed, went behind the bar and into a small stores closet. The bartender, clued in by Yvette, didn't object to this invasion of his workspace.

He sat down on a case of whiskey, glumly remembering his last maladroit conversation with Yvette on the picnic grounds. Luckily, to calm his mind he could rely on his copy of *Mind Control Methods of the Mandarins*.

While he waited, he laid his forearms on his legs, palms upward, closed his eyes, and took three deep breaths.

Yvette returned and laid her tray on a shelf. "What do you want now?"

"I talked to Herr Wong," Sherlock began, "and he said Miss Chung had trained as a riflewoman in the Commune militia."

"Good for her."

"And he said she had a terrible distrust for Molly, who she said was too extreme, trying to take over your group as soon as she arrived."

"Common knowledge," Yvette asserted.

"Maybe it was in your circle."

"So you stop my work to tell me what everyone knows."

Sherlock came out with, "You don't have to talk. Just

give me a headshake. I think I found out a few things that aren't known by everyone. Molly and Miss Chung clashed over when would be the proper time to assassinate Mary Van Winkle."

"Why do you keep calling her that?" Yvette said. "Her name is Yi-Yi. Yi-Yi Chung."

"Yes, that's important," he said thoughtfully. "I should know that."

"Why would anyone fight about killing that woman. Why not just kill her?" she said provocatively.

"Because some of you—"

"Who is 'you'?"

"The ex-Communards got wind of a book Van Winkle was buying for his wife. If you could steal it—and Molly was situated in a good place to steal it, so she had to agree to the plan—you could sell it and help the exiles."

"You, you, you—I'm not connected to all these things," Yvette said.

"I just want one nod," he said.

"Concerning what?"

"My hypothesis. Three days ago, Molly said she was definitely going to knife her mistress at the pump room in the morning. Yi-Yi hid in the corridor to intercept her and they fought. Yi-Yi knocked her over and Molly fell on her knife."

He watched for the nod, but Yvette picked up her tray, straightened her woolly ears, and turned away without giving it.

Chapter 21

While buying tickets to balls didn't come into Marx's tight budget, the fact that Eleanor had splurged with her own money to gather to herself two tickets, one for her, one for the boy, was far from displeasing.

Her choice of companions might have been better. At their early dinner, the conversation was despondent, as everyone seemed to have fallen into themselves. For Marx, it became easier to read their glances than make sense of their words. Cranky kept glancing at a pretty waitress. Sherlock and his daughter were exchanging looks almost of complicity. This last was reassuring, as it suggested the youth had no inkling of Marx's true identity. And Marx was happy to see Eleanor was not mooning over Lissagaray, whose ideas about the Paris Commune Marx often found faulty. Although, with his recent exposure to the intricacies of the Serbian independence movement, Marx was also coming to see weakness in his own views.

He and Engels had adopted a notion of progress, with society going from primitive village communism, where all was share and share alike, through state formation and feudal arrangements to mercantile and then industrial capitalism and then to, they anticipated, the final stage of sophisticated communism.

By contrast, the Serbs were resolutely in favor of holding on to the more distant past. What if society stayed fixed at the beginning, something like the Russian mir, a place of very slowly advancing technology, which still maintained a nonindustrial orientation, held together with mutual aid? And since achievement of such a society was not possible in one go for an already advanced society, as had been attempted in Paris, what about imagining it along the lines of what had happened, though in a negative way, in Serbia? The country had gone backward from a nation of independent peasantry to one of feudal serfdom. Could one, more sanely, begin unplating industrialism to regain the mir's advantages?

There was a knock at the door. Marx lifted himself heavily from the sofa, letting the *Tag* he had been holding but not reading flutter to the carpet.

The door opened to the maid saying, "You left an order for coffee."

It was Swandra.

"I did, yes."

She stepped in, bringing a platter laden with pot, cup, cream, sugar, and spoon, which she carried to a small holding table in front of the sofa, pertly kicking aside the newspaper that blocked her course.

Marx sat back down, tired by the active day and in a state of relaxation after the long hours of balneotherapy. He watched, as much as he could see from behind, the woman's deft movements as, at his request, she mixed in one small spoon of sugar and just the smallest dollop of cream. Earlier in the day he took it black, but now he indulged himself.

From behind, as she leaned to the set, he saw her black uniform was a tad wrinkled, and her russet hair was sieving out from the band on her head.

"Will there be anything else?" she asked, turning to him, crying.

Marx asked the obvious question. "What's wrong?"

She just stood there, tears coming and going at intervals like rain dropping sporadically from branches that had earlier been coated by a storm.

"Perhaps you'd better sit down," he offered.

She plopped down unceremoniously on the far side of the sofa, leaving him near the tray. His arm had been resting on the couch's back, and he moved it a few inches away from her.

"It's just all these murders," she said emotionally.

"I guess your brother's death," Marx offered.

"Estranged brother."

"Yes," he went on. "It's tragic, and no one knows—"

"But what about Captain Von Pelt?" she exclaimed. "He is innocent of all these intrigues. If he hadn't got tangled up with this strumpet ..."

"I know," Marx said. "I wish I could say something that would help you."

"I feel I am talking to someone who has a deep, expressed sympathy for the Serbian fight."

"I? Who am I?" he asked.

"Herr Marx. All the girls know your writing, both about the Serbs and the Commune."

Marx fell back on the sofa. Here was the secret he'd been jealously guarding from the prying intrusions of Sherlock. Turns out he was a byword in every scullery and maids' quarters.

"You know," he told her, "I've written on the Serbian struggles, not flatteringly, but well ..." Perhaps this was not the best path to stanch a maiden's tears, but he was not sure how to handle the situation. "I've stated the Serbs' pursuit of independence is fruitless. If they escaped Austrian tutelage, their freedom would last only as long as it took the czar to invade and swallow them."

She kept shaking and, with a father's unerring intuition, he guessed the sobs were coming from three different places: her nationalist beliefs, her sisterly feelings, and her feelings for Von Pelt. It was very easy for him to come out with his positions on Eastern Europe, such as those he had just reeled off, but alerted by her tears, he resolutely hopped off his high horse and said consolingly, "I can't say I've studied Serbia as completely as I should."

"Understatement."

"So where did I go wrong?" He started to reach for his smoking cup but restrained that impulse.

"You want to upend the system without seeing the worst."

"I'm not—"

"In *Capital*, you mention the English workers expelled from the fields."

"Quite accurate."

"But your England is moving Eastern Europe to the past. It's recreating serfs and slavery to grow its grain. History is at a breaking point, don't you see?"

"Plainly, I don't."

"It's breaking because for England to make progress forward, everyone else has to move backward. Poland back, Hungary back, Serbia back."

Yielding to temptation, Marx picked up his cup, but before bringing it to his lips, he asked, "Why don't you take some coffee. I have another cup somewhere."

She was leaning back further, dislodging a cushion, nodding in the affirmative. "Thank you, milord."

He got up and rummaged till he found a cup that hadn't been returned to the hotel kitchen. He needed to swab it out. He stood looking at his writing desk for something suitable. Swandra got up and bustled over, picking up some tissue from under a book. She took the cup, cleaned it, and returned to the sofa, where she poured coffee and sat down. As Marx came back, she bent and retrieved the newspaper, which she laid on the end table. All this activity seemed to have soothed her.

Marx was thinking, "How can I be diplomatic?" It was not something he was in the habit of asking himself. However, confronting a tearing-up Victorian damsel, he held back his judgment on Serbia's prospects. He put his opinion, saying, "It's true England is wrecking and beggaring the world, but little nation patriotism does not seem fully practical."

It was her turn to concede. "I don't know if our program is realistic. Maybe there is a budget of resistance. People have only limited energy, and if they are mightily oppressed, as we are, they take any possible route to throw it off. Nationalism is just one arrow out."

Marx took another bracing sip of coffee and checked whether more tears were prominent near her powder-blue eyes. A dash of rouge on her cheek was marred by her crying.

He spoke almost apologetically. "I've never doubted the integrity, courage, and selflessness of your Serbian patriots." He recalled this was something he'd said a few days ago about the Poles, but no matter. "From what I've read, your brother was a shining example of this exemplary love of country."

Another minor floodlet. Not his intention at all. Another blocked gesture as he began to bring up his arm from his lap and let it lightly wrap her shoulders in the type of consoling gesture he would have used with Jenny, then stopped himself and let his arm fall to rest on the couch back.

"We all treasured Erick," she told him.

"So why was he poisoned? Who could have done that?" Marx asked. Then, under the inspiration of the moment, Marx thought back to what Cranky had told him in the prison cell. "Maybe I can explain what happened, if that's any solace to you.

"When my friend Dr. Cranky went to assist Fräulein Dussell in the storage building, he was called upstairs, where he found her frantically trying to open the window. It was almost as if she were becoming hysterical, and she a nurse who had served in the war. There were broken glasses on the floor and dust everywhere."

"I know my Erick was hiding there upstairs," she mentioned.

Marx filled in further. "I happened to hear that the attendants at the pump room, those on the last shift, have a checklist of what has to be done every night. They would be severely reprimanded if anything were missed."

"My head is hurting," Swandra said.

Marx kept on, "Just let me connect this. There wouldn't be any glasses missing in the pump room when the morning shift came on. Dussell must have removed them."

"To what point?"

"Let's say," Marx continued, "Dussell went rogue. Without telling any other members of the Serbian group, she decided to kill Henry Van Winkle by bringing him glasses from the storage room laced with the poison colchium. She hurriedly crossed to the upstairs room to put the poison in a glass. Your brother was standing by watching. She dropped the big bottle of poison and it spread everywhere like a fine powder."

"Sounds like she mucked up everything," Swandra noted.

Marx came to the conclusion. "Colchium can kill you by being breathed in. That's why she frantically tried to open the window. But it was too late for your brother Erick. He was overexposured. That's why he ultimately didn't stay hidden when the police were all around. The poison causes a tremendous thirst. He needed to drink."

Marx didn't go on to mention that this explained Kugelmann's last gesture of pointing toward the bookshelf. He was aiming his finger at the water carafe, not at a book.

He felt the need for a second cup of coffee, but the larder was bare. He could only drain a few drops.

Swandra nodded to her own full cup. "I guess I couldn't touch it after all. Whyn't you have it?"

He picked up her cup and took a pull. She hadn't drunk it, but she had smothered it with sugar.

He swigged down her oversweet coffee, dropped the

cup, and patted her on the shoulder. Then, he opened his arms so she could cry again using his shoulder, something Eleanor, in her own tortured independence, could never have brought herself to do.

Chapter 22

Furtively crossing the paving stones in a semideserted section of the main city, deserted because this was ball night, with two other parties on top of the Hunter's shindig, as well as the Wolf-Head Parade, Cranky flitted through the grainy shadows out of the reach of the gas lamps. In the distance, he could hear the guttural sounds of the marching wolves and see the unruly shadows cast by their carried flames.

He had been reading the American Lewis Morgan, who discussed the savages, noble savages, of the East Coast, and then Cranky had gone wider, looking at the Plains tribes. One, the Sioux, had a special birthing ritual, birthing from boy to man, in which the youngster was sent into the desert to hunt, meditate, and seek a vision. He would learn his adult name by finding his adult animal, the one with whom he could commune. The existence of this uncanny double could only be verified by a supremely difficult act of empathy. For a handful of moments, the Sioux brave must skirt along the fringes of the animal's consciousness, using its eyes, its beak, its talons.

Such possibilities of any contact with our animal selves no longer existed. It was the loss of this, along with so many other important traits, such as strength and quick judgment, that Rousseau blamed on the advent of civilization.

Contrast ancients and moderns. The Sioux embarked on a manhood quest, held his breath, and waited. The animal made the approach. It was a lonely and daring one. In Karlsbad, the men egotistically chose what animal, a beast, they admired and to whom they arrogantly and unjustly claimed kinship.

Cranky was thinking, clinging to the shadows near the pump room. He'd managed a few moments alone with Heidi in the bathing facility earlier today, and they'd set this rendezvous where they could talk over their special concerns. They planned to meet in the storage area they'd shared on the morning of the crime, but, its doorway being too well lit for him to wait there, he took temporary refuge on the opposite side, a little down from the pump room, in a souvenir shop entrance.

Heidi was late. He had an eerie feeling, not only because of the distant sounds and spectral flares from the parade, but due to the ring of approaching boots. From the sounds of a whispered conversation, he established two men were coming his way from the far end of the street. They would pass him after they went beyond the pump room.

Should he step out?

They rounded the end of the block, and he made out that one of the men was Pricklestone, close talking with another man he couldn't identify. Cranky was on the brink, undecided. From the way their heads were bowed together, he gauged they would stroll past without glancing his way. He was partly right. They neither glanced at him nor got to him. They stopped and rang the bell to the Feckles domicile. Odd move, given the lights of the third-floor residence were out.

The unknown man bent over as if examining the doorknob, and suddenly the door was keyed up and they were in. The door closed silently behind them.

So, the Pricklestone was a housebreaker.

He had to go to the police, he thought, then modified that: had to go after waiting a few more minutes for Heidi. "What a star-crossed connection we have," he mused. "Whenever we catch a few minutes together, we find there is a crime in progress."

He nailed his eyes to the upstairs drapes and saw them bundled a little closer together by an unseen hand. Probably the same one that held a dark lantern. Cranky was thinking that if he went to look for the police, the two might already have made off before he'd returned. On the other hand, if he awaited Heidi, he could send her to summon the police while he kept watching.

As he looked on, trying and failing to catch sight of something, a twitch of the curtain, perhaps, as a robber scanned the street, he remembered a poem Baudelaire had composed on windows, "Les Fenêtres." The poet was in a mood for paradox. People, he said, exclaim over picturesque holiday sights seen through the windows of their resort hotels, but, in truth, it is looking *in* windows where one captures the greatest views: "Il n'est pas d'objet plus profond, plus mystérieux, plus fécond, plus ténébreux, plus éblouissant qu'une fenêtre éclairée d'une chandelle." (There is no object more deep, mysterious, more fecund and shadowy, more secretive than a window brightened by a single candle.) In illustration, he relates what he sees: "Par dèla des vagues de toits, j'aperçois une femme mûre, ridée déjà, pauvre, toujours penchée sur quelque chose." (Across the waves of roofs, I spy a middle-aged woman, already wrinkled, poor, always bending over something.) Watching her, he creates a delightful fable of her life.

So, Baudelaire, the dandy who wandered like a vagrant, a flâneur, absurdly eavesdropping and peeping along the streets and in the windows of Paris, discovered that there were two distinct sets of emotions belonging to two well-defined groups, the rich and the poor, and that—here is the discovery—one's life is shaped largely by the feelings of the group *to which one does not belong.*

Cranky's thoughts stopped as he heard a light step approach. It's true the discovery of the home invaders had dashed his immediate hopes of a few quiet moments alone with Heidi, but, in recompense, they would be involved in an adventure together. So he was thinking up till he discovered the approacher was not the maid but Eleanor.

He signaled to her, but she nodded and hurried by. Before he could call quietly out to her, Sherlock appeared. The youth was also going to whiz by till Cranky stepped out of the shadows. Even then, he kept walking till the good professor grabbed his forearm.

Sherlock shook him off. "I can't stop now."

"Even to prevent a crime?"

That snatched the boy's attention. "What are you on about?"

Cranky boldly pulled him into a cranny. "I saw Pricklestone break into the Feckleses' building."

Sherlock stepped from the shadows to peer at the building more closely. "It must be the Shakespeare book they are after." After thinking, he continued, "I just passed an officer who is stationed on the side street by the post box. You summon him quickly."

Cranky came back with, "And you?"

"I'll apprehend them," Sherlock said as he flashed his derringer.

Chapter 23

Sherlock's pace up the stairs was muffled, and when he rounded the last landing, his movements became even more subdued on seeing that the thieves, whether through negligence or a desire to warn themselves if there were intrusion from below, had left the apartment door ajar. Although he was pressed for time, he did pause a moment to overhear their conversation.

"Blimey, there's another shelf in this alcove. He's got a lot of books."

"Just check each book, one by one, then put them all back exactly as you found them."

That must be Pricklestone, the brains of the operation.

"Do we even know if they kept the book in the apartment?"

"We don't know anything, but the fish is a very big one if we land it."

They stopped talking and concentrated on searching for their prize. The constant sound of books being withdrawn from and replaced on the shelves made it seem Sherlock were spying on a library.

He slowly went forward, brandishing his weapon, but stopped, startled by the loud voices of massed men who were singing a drinking song. It was the Wolf-Head Parade drawing near.

He went quietly down to the landing and looked out the window, seeing that the marchers were about to round onto this street. But he realized that was unimportant. Using his method of mind-plate capture, which allowed him to take in a full perspective, he had also seen that across the way a man was rooting away on the roof gutters of the pump room. Below him, viewed through the darkened glass sheets of the building, he made out Eleanor slowly ascending the ladder in the back.

Sherlock ran downstairs, not caring about the clatter, and went past Cranky, who was coming up with a police officer. Sherlock must have frightened them as he pounded down the block and streaked past the entrance to the pump room.

Chapter 24

Expecting Sherlock to be right behind her, Eleanor had hurried to the pump room and concealed herself behind the fountain. In less than ten minutes, an intruder showed up, coming not through the entrance but from the buildings behind the pump room. The man climbed the ladder.

What could she do? Their plan depended on two persons being on hand. If the person appeared, one watched while the other summoned the police. Now she was dilemma horned. If she left to get help, the stranger might descend and disappear. All she could do was stand steady below and wait for Sherlock to get here. She waited and watched, her breath snapping in her throat.

She stared upward as the man crossed the glass panels above. His silhouette, overshone by moonlight, let his weak shadow flit over the flagstones below. He was a third of the way out on the roof toward the front when he kneeled and began examining the gutter.

A new thought. If she mounted the ladder and got up to the non-glass-edge portion of the roof, she might be able to detect his identity and then creep back down. There were things in favor of this view. If by some chance, she was discovered—perhaps she might bump into something—he could hardly run across the slippery, half-repaired glass top to lay his hands on her before she could scramble down to safety. Also, consider, this man was not a criminal type, simply a voyeur, so even if he found her out, it was unlikely he would be a menace.

Stealthily, though no more stealthily than a cat, she

crept outdoors into the enclosure and quietly climbed the ladder, her eyes all the time riveted on his furtive movements, which she was seeing as she mounted, looking into and up through two layers of glass. She reached the top and, half bent down, in the posture of a feline about to pounce, took up observation.

Suddenly, in the distance, from behind her, there came a ringing, a singing, and a glow as if a house were afire. It was the marching Wolf-Heads, approaching their block. Their noise caused the intruder to glance toward the origin of the sound and light, which revealed to him a shadowy lump.

"Who's there?" he called out.

It was a signal for her to step away and go back downstairs. She stood up, moving too quickly so that she had to steady herself by stepping onto a pane, which exploded under her sharply placed foot. Next thing, she was piercing the glass, falling through a rent until, halfway down, she was caught by her bustle, which held firm against the roofing. She screamed, a mere trickle of sound against the loud song of the Wolf-Heads.

Lights were generated from the approaching, torch-carrying parade, throwing odd-angled reflections, different on every single pane, spookily shifting. The torches' light played on the man facing her. She was supremely afraid, because the being walking carefully toward her was a gigantic owl.

The owl said, "It's you, Eleanor."

She could almost recognize the voice, but that meant it was someone it never should have been. "Is it you, Dr. Feckles?" she asked.

There was a thin waist of glass between them. He started to advance but stopped when he heard the roofing splinter.

She looked at the weak glass roof and then, looking through it, saw Sherlock running across the floor of the pump room and going out the back door. He would be up the ladder in a jiffy.

Feckles was advancing slowly, scaring her, as the glass roof seemed about to give way altogether. "Can you be careful where you walk?" she asked.

A large cracking sound emphasized her request.

"I don't know why you are spying on me," he said.

"I wanted to find out who was spying on the building across the way," she said nervously.

"And what else do you know?"

That was a telling phrase. He was hiding something. It was either love or country. Either Feckles was keeping tabs on the revolutionaries or trying to find out if his wife was receiving visitors when he was away. It was for her to guess.

"I know your wife had a lover," she hazarded. He seemed a jealous type.

That was the wrong reply, she surmised when she saw him take out a scalpel.

"What are you doing? Just leave," she said plaintively.

She could hear the sound of the paraders who had entered the street. She couldn't wait for them nor for Sherlock if Feckles decided to stab her.

He paused, looking distracted, as if unsure what to say. She made a (finally) disastrous maneuver, trying to break off a wedge of cracked glass, very useful as a weapon, which only succeeded, as her hold slipped, in slashing her elbow. Her blood ran out loosely onto the glass. She pulled down her sleeve to stanch the wound.

Feckles was alert again. "What are you doing?"

"Trying to stop from falling to my death." The glass again nicely backed her words by groaning brittlely. "Listen," she said, "if you shot Von Pelt ..."

That angered him. "You know I didn't kill him. You've figured out too much. You know I caught Van Winkle sneaking up to my wife's room and that I got lost in a jealous fury. It's like one of the elemental forces took me over."

Suddenly the sky blazed as ten, fifteen, twenty torches,

pitched high in the air by the assembled Wolf-Heads on the street below, came crashing down on the roof. It was as if a nearby building had caught fire, sending embers and cinders spinning outward. Red pinwheels were raining all over, bursting holes and cracks in the glass. Each torch, once at rest, smoking and shimmering, sent out wobbly reflections. As new torches fell, the pictures within the separate panes moved and altered, differently dappled, as if each contained the makings of a different dream.

Eleanor, staring ahead, watching and planning, was trying to lift herself, then slipped and made another slit to her arm, spilling more blood.

As far as she could tell with an occasional head twist, Sherlock had stopped at the top of the ladder and was listening, but he was leaving her too exposed. She was about to call his name when she heard him standing up behind her.

"I've heard all I want to hear," the youth said. "Drop your knife on the roof."

"And what's going to stop me, you young whelp?" Feckles taunted.

A shot answered his question.

It winged him and he tumbled backward in a way that in a circus would probably qualify as a professional backflip. He stove through the glass, going head foremost, but by ratcheting out his legs, he managed to trap himself, checking his descent so that his upper torso hung down under the ceiling while his legs fought to hold him aloft, braced on the weakening glass.

Quite a pair. Eleanor, her upper body pinched and stabbed from all sides by the glass she had smashed through, and Feckles, legs aloft, multiply slashed by his passage through the shards. But there was one difference. Snatching off and tearing apart her collar, Tussy force-bandaged the bloody welt on her arm while Feckles, beset by the small torchlit fires eating their way through his head feathers, could not stanch the flow of blood from a gashed thigh, so that the more he shook, the more he poured out his life.

Eleanor felt Sherlock's arms slipping under her armpits as he strained to lift her, but all she could see in front of her—Feckles had fallen to the side, out of her sight line—were the fires and their flashing reflections, as if she were looking on a battle-devastated glass metropolis, a city of drunken angels, that was more beautiful and more destroyed than any that had come before.

∾

Completed: August 11, 2019
Composed: Brooklyn, Guangzhou, Da Nang

"Where is tomorrow?"
—Sun Ra

Acknowledgments

Since I began working on this book in the 1980s, with major intermissions, I have been helped by a lot of people over the years.

Aside from the person to whom this book is dedicated, I would like to thank for their decades of supporting my work (when no one else did), as well as for offering a crash course on the New York jazz scene, on Japanese haiku, and on many other cultural topics, Yuko Otomo and her husband, (the late) Steve Dalachinsky.

For this book, I thank those at PM, particularly Ramsey Kanaan, with his far-seeing vision; Allan Kausch, who not only did the startling cover image, which captures the essence of the book, but in numerous conversations has been a helpful guide to the worlds of surrealism and classic science fiction; and my editor, Cara Hoffman, who sometimes was almost a tutor, suggesting scenes to be added or shifted, which characters could be dropped, and how to pick up the pace of the story, all changes that were of great benefit to the book. Other important helpers were Joey Paxman, Gregory Nipper, and Wade Ostrowski. I must also thank Jonathan Lethem for a wonderful blurb. His works of imagination and passion have been an inspiration to me over the years, from the Dixon Place book party for *Gun, with Occasional Music* and his contributions to *Crank* magazine up till today.

For my understanding of Marx I have to thank Stanley Aronowitz, whose classes at the Grad Center I audited for many semesters. Then there's Michael Pelias, polymath and profound reader of German and French philosophy. Finally, there's Michael Lardner, with whom I was taking a class on *Capital 3* when COVID struck.

Closer to home, I want to thank members of the Unbearables literary group, which formed in the late 1980s. At the head was one of the founders, Peter Lamborn Wilson, who introduced us to Autonomedia Press, whose bighearted publisher, Jim Fleming, published our multiple anthologies and also individual works of the group, including a few of my own titles. Fleming was surrounded by the brilliant thinkers in the Midnight Notes collective, many of whom I came to know, especially Silvia Federici and George Caffentzis. I thank also the writers in the Unbearables group, comrades and collaborators now for thirty-plus years, leading off with Ron Kolm, Carol Wierzbicki, Bonny Finberg, Wanda Phipps, Carl Watson, and Shalom. Also sharing many adventures in the group were Thad Rutkowski, Chavisa Woods, Jason Gallagher, Brenda Guerrero-Gallagher, Meg Kaizu, Hillary Keel, Dorothy Friedman-August, Violet Snow, Sparrow, Jill Rapaport, Michael Randall, Susan Yung, Anna Mockler, Tsuarah Litzky, Bernard Meisler, Tim Beckett, bart plantenga, Rob Hardin, Tom Savage, Michael Carter, David Pemberton, Dave Mandl, Amy Ouzoonian, Arthur Nersesian, Arthur Kaye, Alan Graubard, Amy Barone, Max Blagg, Jordan Zinovich, Eve Packer, Joanna Pagano, Bruce Weber, Vincent Katz, Mike Topp, Dave Huberman, Joe Maynard, Deborah Pintonelli, Lorraine Schein, and Sheila Maldonado.

Outside that group, other writers who have befriended me over the years include Barbara Henning, Lynn Crawford, Clayton Patterson, Valery Oistenau, Donald Nicholson-Smith, Johannah Rogers, Donald Breckenridge, Michael Rothenberg, Jane Oremond, Steve Cannon, Lewis Warsh, Gabriel Don, David Tighe, Kathy Donovan, Eliot Katz, and Gerard Nicosia.

And special encouragement came from friends and sisters Jessica Chu and Vicky Chu (who showed us around Hong Kong) and family members, including our daughter, Ana Cheung, and relatives Mai Mysliwiec, Pui Sun, and Ling Sun (who showed us around Ho Chi Minh City).

My work has appeared in *Fifth Estate* over the years, where founding member of the collective Peter Werbe, no mean journalist and novelist himself, has encouraged me, as has another member, Sylvia Kasdan, activist, writer, and fascinating storyteller.

Going back to college days in the 1970s, I found friends who have stayed close since then: Jerome Sala (I was taking Michael Lardner's classes *Capital 2* and *3* with Jerome as I worked on the book), Elaine Equi, Kevin Riordan, and bassist Matt Dudek.

Lastly, thanks to Richard Brown Lethem, who did the covers for my earlier books and whom I met within a week of stepping off the bus in NYC in 1975.

About the Author

Jim Feast helped found the action-oriented literary group the Unbearables, known for such events as a protest against the commodification of the Beats at NYU's Kerouac Conference, annual readings with poets spread out across the Brooklyn Bridge, and a blindfold tour of the Whitney Museum. In the early 1980s, he met and married Nhi Manh Chung, author of *Among the Boat People*. She introduced him to Chinatown movie theaters, which played the path-breaking Hong Kong noir detective films of those days, giving him a new way to look at the murder mystery. Feast has worked for Fairchild Publications and later taught at Kingsborough Community College. He has edited seven books by Ralph Nader, including his three novels, and worked with Barney Rosset on his autobiography. He lives in Brooklyn.

ABOUT PM PRESS

PM Press is an independent, radical publisher of books and media to educate, entertain, and inspire. Founded in 2007 by a small group of people with decades of publishing, media, and organizing experience, PM Press amplifies the voices of radical authors, artists, and activists.

Our aim is to deliver bold political ideas and vital stories to people from all walks of life and arm the dreamers to demand the impossible. We have sold millions of copies of our books, most often one at a time, face to face. We're old enough to know what we're doing and young enough to know what's at stake. Join us to create a better world.

PM Press
PO Box 23912
Oakland, CA 94623
www.pmpress.org

PM Press in Europe
europe@pmpress.org
www.pmpress.org.uk

FRIENDS OF PM PRESS

These are indisputably momentous times—the financial system is melting down globally and the Empire is stumbling. Now more than ever there is a vital need for radical ideas.

In the many years since its founding—and on a mere shoestring—PM Press has risen to the formidable challenge of publishing and distributing knowledge and entertainment for the struggles ahead. With hundreds of releases to date, we have published an impressive and stimulating array of literature, art, music, politics, and culture. Using every available medium, we've succeeded in connecting those hungry for ideas and information to those putting them into practice.

Friends of PM allows you to directly help impact, amplify, and revitalize the discourse and actions of radical writers, filmmakers, and artists. It provides us with a stable foundation from which we can build upon our early successes and provides a much-needed subsidy for the materials that can't necessarily pay their own way. You can help make that happen—and receive every new title automatically delivered to your door once a month—by joining as a Friend of PM Press. And, we'll throw in a free T-shirt when you sign up.

Here are your options:

- **$30 a month** Get all books and pamphlets plus a 50% discount on all webstore purchases

- **$40 a month** Get all PM Press releases (including CDs and DVDs) plus a 50% discount on all webstore purchases

- **$100 a month** Superstar—Everything plus PM merchandise, free downloads, and a 50% discount on all webstore purchases

For those who can't afford $30 or more a month, we have **Sustainer Rates** at $15, $10 and $5. Sustainers get a free PM Press T-shirt and a 50% discount on all purchases from our website.

Your Visa or Mastercard will be billed once a month, until you tell us to stop. Or until our efforts succeed in bringing the revolution around. Or the financial meltdown of Capital makes plastic redundant. Whichever comes first.

RUIN
Cara Hoffman

ISBN: 978-1-62963-929-1 (paperback)
    978-1-62963-931-4 (hardcover)
$14.95/$25.95   128 pages

A little girl who disguises herself as an old man, an addict who collects dollhouse furniture, a crime reporter confronted by a talking dog, a painter trying to prove the non-existence of god, and lovers in a penal colony who communicate through technical drawings—these are just a few of the characters who live among the ruins. Cara Hoffman's short fictions are brutal, surreal, hilarious, and transgressive, celebrating the sharp beauty of outsiders and the infinitely creative ways humans muster psychic resistance under oppressive conditions. RUIN is both bracingly timely and eerily timeless in its examination of an American state in free-fall: unsparing in its disregard for broken, ineffectual institutions, while shining with compassion for the damaged left in their wake. The ultimate effect of these ten interconnected stories is one of invigoration and a sense of possibilities—hope for a new world extracted from the rubble of the old.

Cara Hoffman is the author of three New York Times Editors' Choice novels; the most recent, *Running*, was named a Best Book of the Year by *Esquire Magazine*. She first received national attention in 2011 with the publication of *So Much Pretty* which sparked a national dialogue on violence and retribution, and was named a Best Novel of the Year by the *New York Times Book Review*. Her second novel, *Be Safe I Love You*, was nominated for a Folio Prize, named one of the Five Best Modern War Novels, and awarded a Sundance Global Filmmaking Award. A MacDowell Fellow and an Edward Albee Fellow, she has lectured at Oxford University's Rhodes Global Scholars Symposium and at the Renewing the Anarchist Tradition Conference. Her work has appeared in the *New York Times, Paris Review, BOMB, Bookforum, Rolling Stone, Daily Beast*, and on NPR. A founding editor of the *Anarchist Review of Books*, and part of the Athens Workshop collective, she lives in Athens, Greece, with her partner.

"RUIN *is a collection of ten jewels, each multi-faceted and glittering, to be experienced with awe and joy. Cara Hoffman has seen a secret world right next to our own, just around the corner, and written us a field guide to what she's found. I love this book.*"
—Sara Gran, author of *Infinite Blacktop* and *Claire Dewitt and the City of the Dead*

23 Shades of Black

Kenneth Wishnia
with an introduction by
Barbara D'Amato

ISBN: 978-1-60486-587-5
$17.95   300 pages

23 Shades of Black is socially conscious crime
fiction. It takes place in New York City in the
early 1980s, i.e., the Reagan years, and was
written partly in response to the reactionary
discourse of the time, when the current thirty-year assault on the rights
of working people began in earnest, and the divide between rich and
poor deepened with the blessing of the political and corporate elites. But
it is not a political tract, it's a kick-ass novel that was nominated for the
Edgar and the Anthony Awards, and made *Booklist*'s Best First Mysteries
of the Year.

The heroine, Filomena Buscarsela, is an immigrant who experienced
tremendous poverty and injustice in her native Ecuador, and who grew
up determined to devote her life to helping others. She tells us that she
really should have been a priest, but since that avenue was closed to
her, she chose to become a cop instead. The problem is that as one
of the first *latinas* on the NYPD, she is not just a woman in a man's
world, she is a woman of color in a white man's world. And it's hell.
Filomena is mistreated and betrayed by her fellow officers, which leads
her to pursue a case independently in the hopes of being promoted to
detective for the Rape Crisis Unit.

Along the way, she is required to enforce unjust drug laws that she
disagrees with, and to betray her own community (which ostracizes her
as a result) in an undercover operation to round up illegal immigrants.
Several scenes are set in the East Village art and punk rock scene of
the time, and the murder case eventually turns into an investigation of
corporate environmental crime from a working class perspective that is
all-too-rare in the genre.

And yet this thing is damn funny, too.

"Packed with enough mayhem and atmosphere for two novels."
—*Booklist*

Critique of the Gotha Program

Karl Marx
with an Introduction by Peter Hudis
and a Foreword by Peter Linebaugh

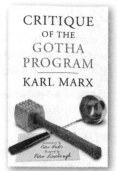

ISBN: 978-1-62963-916-1
$15.95   156 pages

Marx's *Critique of the Gotha Program* is a
revelation. It offers the fullest elaboration of
his vision for a communist future, free from the shackles of capital, but
also the state. Neglected by the statist versions of socialism, whether
Social Democratic or Stalinist that left a wreckage of coercion and
disillusionment in their wake, this new annotated translation of Marx's
Critique makes clear for the first time the full emancipatory scope of
Marx's notion of life after capitalism. An erudite new introduction by
Peter Hudis plumbs the depth of Marx's argument, elucidating how
his vision of communism, and the transition to it, was thoroughly
democratic. At a time when the rule of capital is being questioned
and challenged, this volume makes an essential contribution to a real
alternative to capitalism, rather than piecemeal reforms. In the twenty-
first century, when it has never been more needed, here is Marx at his
most liberatory.

"*This is a compelling moment for a return to Marx's most visionary writings.
Among those is his often neglected,* Critique of the Gotha Program. *In
this exciting new translation, we can hear Marx urging socialists of his day
to remain committed to a truly radical break with capitalism. And in Peter
Hudis's illuminating introductory essay we are reminded that Marx's vision
of a society beyond capitalism was democratic and emancipatory to its very
core. This book is a major addition to the anti-capitalist library.*"
—David McNally, Distinguished Professor of History, University of
Houston and author of *Monsters of the Market*

"*In their penetrating account of Marx's famous hatchet job on the 19th-
century left, Hudis and Anderson go to the heart of issues haunting the left
in the 21st century: what would a society look like without work, wages,
GDP growth, and human self-oppression.*"
—Paul Mason, writer for *New Statesman* and author of *Postcapitalism: A
Guide to Our Future*